KALEIDOSCOPE

Venus Reising

BELLA
BOOKS
2019

Bella Books, Inc.
P.O. Box 10543
Tallahassee, FL 32302

Printed in the United States of America on acid-free paper.

First Bella Books Edition 2019

Editor: Ann Roberts
Cover Designer: Judith Fellows

ISBN: 978-1-64247-013-0

Other Bella Books By Venus Reising

Ruthless
Sculpting Anna

Acknowledgements

Thank you to the wonderful women at Bella Books without whom our dream of being storytellers would be just that—a dream. And thank you to the fabulous author and editor, Ann Roberts, for helping us to find our many loose and frayed plot threads and the far too many *still's* in our manuscript. Ann, we promise that things will not be so still in future books. We'd also like to thank our families for their abundance of love and support and, of course, for giving us toys like Wacky WallWalkers that we could later use in silly analogies in our novels. Thank you, too, to the interesting people with whom we have crossed paths for inspiring characters and plotlines. And finally and most importantly, thank you, dear readers, for spending an afternoon with our stories.

About the Author

Venus Reising is the alter ego of a writing duo out of Orlando, Florida. The literary twosome is one-half professor, with poetry and criticism published in numerous journals, including *Ascent Aspirations*, *Falling Star* and *Atlantic Literary Review*, and one-half working artist turned psychology student, who has, at least for now, traded her canvas for a *DSM-5*. The Venus women would much rather interrogate characters and complicate plots than do just about anything else.

Dedication

According to the FBI's "Hate Crime Statistics" report, the incidences of hate crimes in 2017 increased by 17% since the previous year. Sixty percent of the victims were targeted because of their race, ethnicity, or ancestry. We dedicate this book to the victims and to the organizations and people who serve them.

CHAPTER ONE

His voice rose above the cacophony of the distant airboat motors. "You better run little piggy!" A single gunshot punctuated the sentence. She ducked out of instinct or fear, she wasn't sure which. Judging by the sound, though, he'd shot straight up into the sky from back where he'd started the counting.

Weeds slashed her ankles and shins as she raced for the river. The tall grasses that blended into the canopy of low-hanging tree moss obscured everything beyond just a few feet. Tiny diamonds of sunlight shone intermittently through the thick blades. Her heart leapt into a panic as she mistook each glint for the gold bill of his New Orleans Saints ball cap.

She stopped to catch her breath and strained to hear past the hum of the motors and the blood pounding in her own ears. Sweat stung her eyes. She fought the urge to close them. The fields were silent. Nothing. *Had she lost him?* Just before relief could take hold, his voice cracked through the still calm like lightning.

"She goes, 'wee wee, wee,'" he said, "all the way home!"

He was close now. She could hear the barking of the dogs. She pushed harder through the wiry grasses, her hands and knees slipping like eels in the dark, wet dirt.

And then she saw it—a clearing up ahead. *Almost there.* The mud grew softer and deeper the closer she got. She was slipping. Sliding. Struggling to keep her momentum.

She reached her arm toward her reflection in the water, as if the watery image could grab hold of the real her and swim them both to safety. But the watery her wasn't *her* at all. It was a girl in pigtails, less than half her age. The girl stared back at her from the surface—eyes wild, hair a tangle. Before Shae could even process what she was seeing, her dress collar was yanked and she was choking. Coughing. Her fingers helplessly, futilely struggled to free her throat from the fabric tourniquet.

"Gotcha!" His voice sounded giddy and childish, as if it belonged in a game of tag at recess—its inappropriateness both monstrous and disturbing.

With one hand still gripping her collar, he used the other to yank her pigtails, sending the pink, beaded ponytail holder flying like one of those little rubber bands the kids flick from their braces in gym class. Her body crashed against his tree-trunk-size, blue-jeaned thigh. The stench of moonshine, motor oil, and sweat assaulted her nostrils. As she strained to free herself, her hair follicles cried out, and her mind filled with those terrible cinematic images of leathery Indian scalps dangling from saddles like animal pelt trophies—the scalp's dark hair horrifically animated by the gallop of the horses. One of the dogs snarled at her, its muscular body a tight coil, its teeth menacingly bared. She instinctively squeezed her eyes shut and flinched away from its hot breath and intimidating growl.

"You got it wrong, little piggy," the man said. "*I'm* the one to be scared of." The red handkerchief tied around his nose and mouth jerked up and down with his sardonic laughter.

A woman's voice spiraled toward her from somewhere else—somewhere above or outside of this place.

"Shae. Wake up, Shae. Wake up."

She blinked and the grasslands transformed into a quilt of green, yellow, and white-patterned squares. She was in bed—her bed. She drew the cool air-conditioned air in through her nostrils and let it fill her throat, which was, only moments before, too constricted to allow the escape of even the hint of a scream. She surveyed the outline of her sheeted body. She was taller...older.

"You cried out," her mother said.

Shae reached up and felt her short natural curls with her palms. "I had pigtails."

"*You?* No." Her mother laughed. "Braids maybe, never pigtails." She was right of course. Shae had never worn her hair in pigtails—too easily caught by the branches of trees she was climbing or yanked by the fingers of boys with whom she was sparring. She'd never been one for dresses either. And definitely never pink. That girl wasn't her. And yet somehow *she was*.

"You must've had a nightmare."

"A nightmare," Shae repeated with the man's voice still echoing in her ears and the smell of his rank sweat stubbornly clinging to her nostrils. She stretched her right leg out of the sheet to inspect the stinging cuts and scrapes on her ankles and calves. It was pristine. Unmarked. "Must've been," she said.

"I thought for sure you'd be up by now." Her mother squinted at the absurdly large watch on her wrist.

The night of her father's funeral two years earlier, Shae had found her mother struggling to use an old pair of gardening sheers to cut an extra hole in the leather strap, her eyes swimming in tears, her fingers trembling. "I just want to...feel him. Near me," her mother had said, the strength of her voice choking and sputtering like an engine with a clogged carburetor. Shae had felt it too, the gaping hole that had opened in his absence—a hole so large that she expected it to consume the farmhouse like those black holes on the Science Channel that swallowed the stars.

Shae watched the corners of her mother's lips lift into a half-smile, her gaze still fixed to the compass-size timepiece.

She wasn't reading the time; she was traveling through time, turning its pages back to a chapter before the hole had taken up residence in their home and in their hearts. Shae could almost see her father in his blue overalls with the worn knees, his square chin darkened with scruff and dirt from the fields, laughing his belly laugh that finished in a wheezing cough. Her throat swelled at the memory.

"Isn't today the day that Fernanda comes home?" her mother asked.

Shae shrugged, as if to say, "Yeah, so?" or, "Oh, yeah? Is today that day? I'd forgotten."

Of course she hadn't forgotten. In fact, she'd been counting down the days ever since her mother had shared the news at dinner as nonchalantly as if remarking on the weather. It was right in between asking Shae if she could pass the potatoes and instructing her to bring the old Chrysler Imperial in for a tune-up. "Oh, and that old girlfriend of yours," she'd said, "She's coming to spend the summer at Ruby's." *That old girlfriend of yours.*

Shae's cheeks had immediately heated, her mind filling with the image of a seven-year-old Fern preparing to blow the seeds off a dandelion, her pink lips plumped into a pout and her pretty blue eyes squeezed shut in concentration.

"What're you wishing for?" she had asked Fern all those years ago.

"I wished I could stay here forever," Fern had said and leaned into Shae's arms. Shae remembered how the seeds had caught the light like fairy dust in the perfectly blue and still sky, more perfect than she could ever remember it being since.

But Fern couldn't stay there forever. The future Fern's parents had in mind for her was in Manhattan, with its elite private schools and its streets paved with opportunity and promise.

While the Beaumonts and the Williamses had lived close enough for the girls to bike back and forth between each other's houses, when it came to money, they might as well have been on different continents. Of course, like any third grader, Shae was as oblivious to class barriers as she was to heartbreak. So as she had watched the Beaumonts' car disappear into the horizon for a final time, she understood none of that. All she knew was that she felt as though she might suffocate under the weight of her own sadness.

"I'll write," Fern had promised as she'd tied the friendship bracelet around Shae's wrist. "Real letters and they'll go on a great adventure, traveling from state to state until they find their way to you."

For several weeks, Shae had checked the mailbox religiously, practically mauling the postman before he'd even made it to the neighbor's property. But there were never any letters—real or otherwise—from Fern.

And now it had been ten years since they'd seen each other, ten years since they'd lain on their backs in the grass tracing pictures in the clouds, ten years since they'd pricked their fingers with safety pins and sworn an oath of friendship in their makeshift fort of scavenged construction site scraps. A lot had changed in ten years. Fern was in college now.

"Studying aquatic biology at Syracuse," Ruby had told her.

And Shae? Shae was working at the local watering hole and serving a Louisiana delicacy, gator bites, to tourists. She and Fern probably had nothing in common now. It'd be a miracle if Fern even remembered her. But she sure remembered Fern.

"But Grandma doesn't even have cable!" Fern used her index finger to trace a frown in the misted glass of the car window.

"It'll be good for you to... Oh, what do they call that?" her mother asked as she rummaged through her purse. Fern knew what she was looking for. If there was such a thing as a gum addiction, her mother had it. A fresh pack opened in the morning was sure to be empty by noon.

"Going off the grid?" her father offered.

"Unplugging, I think," her mother continued, seeming not to hear him. Fern could hear the crinkling of a gum wrapper.

"This is a good opportunity for you to get serious and focus on your studies, Fernanda. You need to get your head back in the game."

Fern rolled her eyes. Sure she'd partied, but that's what people do in college. The best years of her life, right? And she would have had a B if that jackass Dr. Summers hadn't docked her two letter grades for attendance.

"College isn't cheap, you know," her mother said. "And there's almost nothing you can do these days without a college degree. Isn't that right, Harry?" Without even waiting for a nod of his head, she continued. "It's about maturity, responsibility, character…"

Fern wasn't listening anymore. She'd heard the "education is important" speech enough times to recite it by rote. She turned her attention instead to the scenery. An old rusted Chevy truck propped on cinder blocks. The hand-painted sign attached to its windshield read: Hot boiled pee-nuts. Fish. Bait. *Pee-nuts?* How was she ever going to survive the summer in this *Deliverance* place?

But she *had* actually survived there—for nine years. Before Manhattan they'd lived in St. Charles Parish on the banks of the Mississippi, less than twenty miles from the Chevy on the cinder blocks. Her father, a member of a large, residential energy company's board of directors, had a salary comparable to most university operating budgets. So saying that they lived comfortably was an understatement.

Like the rest of the country, the parish of her childhood was not immune to inequities. The antebellum architecture of the historic mansions, like theirs, was a huge tourist attraction, but a third of parish inhabitants struggled to make do with incomes barely above the poverty line. The filthy rich and the downtrodden were practically neighbors.

When Fern was young, she hadn't noticed the differences, never once considering why some of her schoolmates had reduced-price lunch tokens and had to borrow clothes for phys ed. She wished that she could *not* notice now as they passed the fifth abandoned farm, its windows boarded up, and its arid fields the color of decay. An old rusty tractor sat in the center of it all, the headlamps covered by a thick layer of grime, as if it had long ago closed its lids to the wasted potential all around. On the other side of the property's wire fence, the grass was greener—literally. The neighboring farm was lush and vibrant with rows upon rows of sugarcane plants softly bending in the breeze. And the dormer windows of the large French colonial were positioned such that they seemed to be critically appraising the much less fortunate neighbors with an aloof condescension.

Fern already hated it there and not just because the poverty made her feel guilty for being born into a family that could afford such conveniences as a cleaning service and private chef. Everything was slow here, including the people. When they'd stopped at the general store for a bathroom break, she'd had trouble navigating through the throngs of locals chatting it up with the owner about some new pickled beets recipe. *What is it with pickling things in the South anyway?* Fern made a face.

"...And the one thing that no one can take away from you," her mother continued, "is knowledge." She snapped her gum for effect.

"I know," Fern mumbled, adding a goatee to the frowning face in the window glass. This was not the summer she had in mind. She'd still packed the cute La Perla bikini she'd bought for the beach parties in the Hamptons. She could at least look good sunbathing. Then again, if there's no one there but her grandmother to notice, why bother?

Fern hadn't actually seen her grandmother since they'd left Louisiana. Her father had tried to get Ruby to come to New York for Thanksgiving, but she'd declined, noting what she called, "an allergy to subways, tall buildings and corporate greed." To be honest, Fern wasn't looking forward to the reunion.

Her grandmother's one-story farmhouse looked just like she remembered with the open-ended central hall flanked by two cabins under the same roof, two brick chimneys on either side poking up into the sky like bug antennae.

"What do they call these houses again?" Fern asked.

"Dogtrot," her dad said as he pulled the car to a stop in the gravel driveway. "Because of the breezeway in the center."

Her mother deposited her barely chewed gum in a balled-up tissue, dropped it in the console side pocket, and then went looking for another piece. "I think they were called dog run houses," she said as if she hadn't heard him.

"That so?" her dad asked, winking at Fern.

As her father maneuvered Fern's designer Cartier suitcases out of the trunk, the farmhouse's screen door elicited an angry creak that pulled her gaze to the house and her grandmother. Ruby Beaumont was in her mid-to-late sixties now, which to Fern meant liver spots, Meals on Wheels, and walkers with tennis ball feet. But this woman practically danced down the walkway, the strings of glass beads and shells around her neck noisily clacking against each other with every step.

Before Fern knew what was happening, she was suffocated in her grandmother's ample bosom, which, to her surprise, smelled more like patchouli than mothballs. The woman had apparently bathed in the stuff, the scent so pungent that it made Fern's eyes water.

"Little Fernanda," her grandmother cooed.

"Not so little anymore," her father said.

"Let me have a look at you," her grandmother said, taking a step back. "My goddess! You're stunning." *Goddess?* "I bet you're breaking hearts all over the place!"

Fern shrugged with what she hoped was enough disinterest to warrant a change of subject. To be honest, she wished that were true, not that she wanted to break people's hearts, but she wished there was someone into her enough to feel heartbroken if she wasn't interested back.

"Why, the last time I saw you," Ruby continued, "you were just a little thing, all knees and elbows." Turning to Fern's father now, she said, "I'll never forgive you, Harry, for keeping her away this long."

He planted a kiss on her cheek. "I missed you too, Momma."

While her mother and father disappeared down a hallway with the suitcases, Fern was ushered into the kitchen.

"How about some iced tea, dear? It's a real scorcher today." Ruby's head vanished behind the refrigerator door.

Fern glanced at the open windows. The sheer lace curtains lay flat in the oppressive and stagnant heat. "You don't have air conditioning?"

Her grandmother emerged, pitcher in hand. "The fossil fuels," she said, her forehead crinkled like an accordion. "With your environmental science studies, I'm sure you—"

"Aquatic biology," Fern corrected. She didn't want to be mixed up with those dread-headed, granola crunchers who bragged about their nano-size ecological footprints and made offensive art out of Keurig K-cups. *The environuts.*

It wasn't that Fern didn't care about the environment. She felt the normal twinges of guilt when drinking from plastic water bottles or slipping one of those cardboard sleeves onto her morning Starbucks latte. But she definitely wasn't fanatical enough to chain herself to a redwood or spend her trust fund on ghee from pasture-raised cows.

It was neither a love of nature nor science that led her to aquatic biology. Ironically enough, she'd chosen her major because it reminded her of the bayou of her childhood. The summer days that she and her best friend had spent in the marshy lakes and wetlands, trying to catch bream, perch, and carp with just their hands, racing turtles on the trails, and swinging like monkeys from tree vines. Those times were special to her because they were filled with a joy and wonder unlike any she'd experienced since. And while she quickly grew to prefer the fast paced, rich culture, and beauty of New York's graffitied cityscape, a piece of her heart had remained in the Louisiana bayou of her youth.

"Yes, yes, aquatic biology, of course. That's what I meant," Ruby said.

"So no central air then?"

Ruby frowned and set a glass in front of her. "Not to worry, dear. I put one of those window units in your bedroom so you're comfortable." She poured the tea from the pitcher into Fern's glass. "And we have plenty of fans."

Fern glanced at the stovetop percolator that looked like some kind of archeological relic. She'd go into Nespresso withdrawal for sure! She clicked on the Starbucks locator app on her iPhone and waited for the spinning circle to disappear. It didn't. No Service. *Crap.* "Are you still offline?"

"Off what?"

"You know, do you have Wi-Fi?" Seeing her grandmother's puzzled look, she added, "For the Internet. I can plug in if it's an Ethernet connection and—"

"I'm sorry, dear, but I've never had a need for all that AOL 'you've got mail' stuff. Regular mail works just fine."

AOL? "There's got to be a Starbucks that has Wi-Fi, though, right? There's one on every corner."

"We have Joe's Newsstand and Coffee."

No Netflix streaming, no Facebook, no Twitter, no Instagram, no YouTube, no central air, and no lattes? Could it be any worse? Fern tasted her iced tea and gagged. "Is there sugar?"

"Oh, no, I don't keep refined white sugar in the house. That stuff will kill you. But I'll pick up some date sugar next time I'm at the farmer's market."

Yep, it can be worse.

CHAPTER TWO

Shae could feel the heat of the pavement through the soles of her sneakers as she half-sat and half-stood on the scooter's seat and watched the Beaumont house from what she hoped was a safe enough distance away to not be seen. What made her stop was the unfamiliar car in the driveway, one of those crossover SUVs that was far too much of a gas-guzzler for Ruby's conscience. No sign of Fern, though.

When her phone vibrated in her pocket, she knew exactly who it was. Practically everyone she knew preferred texting to calling, everyone except her boss, Desi. The man was so behind the times that they still used handwritten carbon-backed guest checks. She was late for her shift and it was just about the time for their weekly beer delivery. Des was no doubt irritated to be talking to her voice mail while struggling to seat guests, cook the food, serve the dishes, and see to the delivery, all at the same time. Her guilt got the better of her and she pushed the kill switch into the run position. A commotion at the farmhouse stopped her from hitting the start button.

She saw Ruby first and then a middle-age couple with a young blonde in tow. "I know, I know," the blonde said. "Don't waste the opportunity. Focus on my studies. Got it."

Fern.

She was beautiful, her porcelain skin sun-kissed and dusted with freckles, her blond hair resting in layers on her sexy bare shoulders.

"Mind your grandmother," Mr. Beaumont said.

"If you promise to bring me a trenta mocha latte on your next visit, I will."

"Deal."

Shae waited for the car to pull out of the driveway and for the women to disappear into the house before starting the scooter's engine. Desi was already pissed. Another five minutes wouldn't change anything, she reasoned, as she turned her scooter into the Beaumont driveway.

"Shae!" A smiling Ruby held the door open with her palm. "What a nice surprise! Come in!"

"I just thought I'd stop and say hi on my way to work."

"I'm so glad you did! Fernanda is visiting for the summer and she just arrived this afternoon."

"Oh, yeah? That's nice."

"Yes, yes, it is." Ruby motioned her in. "You two were close when you were kids. I'm sure she'd love to see you."

"We were really little. She probably doesn't—" The sight of Fern walking into the living room on those legs that seemed to stretch on forever stopped her mouth and made her heart thrum so fast and hard that she feared Ruby would hear it.

"Hi Fern," Shae managed through a suddenly dry mouth. "I don't know if you remember me, but when we were kids…" The words seemed to get lost somewhere in the distance between them. Shae had the inexplicable desire to move closer to find them again.

Fern stared, eyes wide, lips slightly parted. After a beat, she whispered, "Shae?"

Shae nodded dumbly into the silence, which grew more awkward with each passing second.

"Well," Ruby said, startling Shae. Somehow she'd forgotten that there was anyone there besides Fern and her. "I see you two have some catching up to do. I'll just get us all some iced tea."

"Oh, thank you, Ruby, but I can't stay. I have…" Shae tried to be polite and look at Ruby, but her gaze wouldn't leave Fern. "…work."

"It's really you?" Fern asked.

"It's been a while, right? How've you been, Fern?"

"Good. I'm good." She smiled, her cheeks noticeably pinker than before. "I'm going to Syracuse, but I'm doing the summer school thing at the community college here." She rolled her eyes. "What a joke, right?"

Shae nodded even though she didn't think the community college was a joke at all. In fact, she'd been saving what money she could to enroll there.

"What about you?" Fern asked.

Not knowing what to do with her hands, Shae slid them into the pockets of her jeans. "I skipped college…for now anyway." She stared at her shoes, embarrassment heating her neck and cheeks.

"Good thinking."

Confused, Shae looked up.

"You don't have to waste your summer making up a class you failed because you knew enough to pass it without going," Fern laughed. "Apparently what matters isn't what you learn. It's whether you show up to listen to the professor drone on and on about his cat."

Shae's cheeks were beginning to ache from smiling so much. Her pocket vibrated with what she imagined to be an angrier and more insistent message than before. *How long have I been here?* She glanced at her watch. *Ten minutes already?* "It's great to catch up, Fern, but I really have to get going."

"Where do you work?"

"A hole in the wall actually named Hole in the Wall." She laughed nervously, trying to hide her embarrassment.

"Does this Hole in the Wall have Wi-Fi?"

"'Fraid not, but we do have darts."

"Well, that doesn't sound half bad given that my dream of binge-watching *Orange Is the New Black* is obviously not going to be realized." She held up her iPhone. "This might as well be a paperweight."

"Season three?"

"Yeah."

"Haven't met Ruby Rose yet then?"

She shook her head.

"You're in for a treat." The confused expression on Fern's face made her want to reel the words back in. Of course Ruby Rose wouldn't be a treat for a straight girl like Fern—the girl who, in the photograph attached to Ruby's refrigerator, was dressed in that sexy, strapless ivory gown. She looked elated to be enclosed in the tuxedoed arms of a tall, handsome surfer-looking boy. "I mean," she said, "it's an interesting plot twist." *Interesting plot twist? Do you write for* TV Guide, *Shae?*

"Well, I hope so. I'm getting really bored with Alex. I was hoping Piper would get a new love interest this season…"

Shae barely heard her. She couldn't help but dwell on the photo—Fern in her prom dress with her handsome boyfriend and his unkempt bangs.

"So, maybe I'll come by Hole in the Wall later."

Something like sadness or jealousy bubbled up inside Shae. And before she could stop it, a caustic, "Yeah, whatever," fell off her tongue.

Fern's smile dissolved and Shae felt terrible for having been the cause. They hadn't seen each other since third grade and here she was acting like some kind of jilted lover. And for no reason. Fern didn't know she'd harbored these feelings for her all these years. How could she? She'd never told her. She didn't even know she was gay. "I mean, of course I'd love for you to come," she said and forced a smile.

Fern hesitated and studied her. Shae felt distinctly uncomfortable under her steady gaze and couldn't help but look away. She focused on the curtains instead.

"Okay then. I'll bring my dart face."

"Poker face. No such thing as a dart face."

"How can you say that when you haven't seen mine yet?" Shae laughed. "As cute as ever." She hadn't meant to say it aloud. In fact, she didn't know that she had until she saw Fern's eyebrows raise in question. A trickle of sweat slid down Shae's spine. Her face felt like it was on fire. In fact, her whole body was an inferno. She wiped her damp palms on her jeans. "Well, I really have to run," she said and turned toward the door.

As she slung her leg over the scooter seat and fumbled with her keys, she heard Fern's voice from behind her. She wasn't sure but she thought she heard her say, "I've missed you." When she turned, the door was already closed and Fern was nowhere in sight. *Probably imagined it.*

Fern was bored and she hadn't even been there two full hours. Now that she'd finished unpacking her suitcase, hanging her blouses in the closet, and stacking the rest of her clothes in the empty dresser drawers, she wasn't sure what to do. She was starting to feel claustrophobic. The little room had barely enough space for the twin bed, the dresser, and the single nightstand— let alone her suitcases and books. There was nothing else in the room except for a solitary lamp, an alarm clock that repeatedly flashed twelve o'clock despite it being close to four, and a box of tissues. One window was obscured by an air conditioner unit that seemed incapable of blowing a stream of cool air wider than a popsicle stick. She leaned toward it and felt what little relief she could as the tiny air stream attempted unsuccessfully to lift her bangs off her forehead.

The wood floor creaked under her bare feet, drawing her attention to the silence. So unlike what she was used to. Her dorm was alive with the almost electric hum of voices all speaking at once, the meditative sounds of the hairdryers in the background, the occasional explosive car crashes and gunshots from the lounge's television speakers, and the slap of ping-pong balls in the rec room. And before college, there had been

Manhattan—the car horns, screeching tires, the loud drunken shouts after the bars let out, and the dance music that, from a distance, dissolved into a thrumming bass that pulsed inside her bones. The constant noise was comforting.

She checked her Apple Watch. Four o'clock. The girls would have arrived in Southampton hours ago. Instead of sipping a cappuccino at Sant Ambroeus or trying on cute outfits at Saks, she was stuck in an episode of *Little House on the Prairie*. Date sugar. Fans. Percolators. She wouldn't be surprised if her grandmother took their clothes to the river to beat them with wooden sticks and rocks.

She left the claustrophobic little room in search of... anything to do. Framed photographs decorated the hallway. She recognized her father's chin in a black and white photo of a little boy in a firefighter's helmet. He was pedaling a tricycle, his face tight with concentration. And then there was her father in a tuxedo, his smiling lips smeared with icing. Her mother, looking beautiful and young, stood at his side, her delicate hands shielding her laughter from his view. Fern couldn't help but marvel at the joy and love housed in that five-by-seven frame. Her parents had married at nineteen, her age now. The thought made her chest heavy. She wanted the happily ever after. She wanted her very own icing-smeared Prince Charming. While she'd been out on lots of dates, she'd never felt what her mother described as, "the world falling away until there's nothing but you and him and an unmistakable electricity." Unless of course electricity meant boredom. She'd definitely felt that. The creak of the floor must have announced her presence because Ruby poked her head out of one of the rooms.

"All unpacked?" she asked, the soft skin around her eyes and lips creasing into deep half-moons.

"Yeah." Fern forced a smile. "What are you up to?"

"Come and see."

The room was some sort of studio. A jungle of shelves were filled with old jelly jars and plastic containers of paint tubes and brushes, what looked to be PVC piping of different lengths, and clear bins filled with colorful and shiny things, like pipe cleaners, sequins and rolled felt. Centered below the only window was a worktable covered in strips of mirrored glass and more piping. "What's all this?" she asked motioning to the glass.

"I've been making kaleidoscopes." Ruby wiped her hands on a towel. She opened a wooden cupboard and reached inside for one of several shoeboxes stacked on the shelves. She handed the box to her.

Packed inside a foam insert was a tube painted in swirling oranges, yellows, purples, and greens that reminded her of the images of Woodstock she'd seen in her school textbooks. A large metal ornament of colored glass pieces was affixed to its end.

She ran her finger along the ornate copper wiring wound around the piece like ivy. "It's beautiful."

"Much more beautiful through the eyepiece." Ruby pointed to its end.

She pressed the tube to her eye and the world came to life in a pinwheel of colored diamond shapes, an intricate pattern that reminded her of those beautiful bidjar rugs she'd seen in the Indian marketplace bazaar on the Travel Channel. She turned the tube clockwise and watched the diamonds transform into softer, rounder shapes like flower petals—a lotus of sparkling turquoise, emerald, and sapphire gems.

"Just a slight move and the whole world changes," Ruby said.

With another turn, the flower petals changed into what looked like musical scales.

"It's magical." Fern said.

"Oh yes, it is. I think you'll find that when you change the way you look at something, the thing itself changes."

"Hey, baby doll! Settle a bet for us and lift that shirt of yours. Frank here thinks you're going commando."

Ignoring the drunken voice from the far end of the bar, Shae forced a smile and focused on what she was doing. She set the steaming plate of clam fritters and a basket of shrimp down on the heavily laminated tabletop.

"Can I get you two anything else?" she asked the couple. The woman glanced at the bar and then smiled sympathetically into her shrimp basket.

"Get your pretty ass over here!" The voice boomed so loudly this time that Shae thought she heard some of the glasses clatter on the bar shelves. Instinctively, her fingers curled into tight fists. She dug her fingernails into the meat of her palms to keep them from acting on the impulse to clamp around the guy's throat and squeeze the male machismo out of his arteries like toothpaste. Instead, she wiped her hands on the bistro apron at her waist, gritted her teeth, and exhaled noisily through her nostrils.

"What, you deaf or something? Sexy and deaf. Wouldn't that be the perfect combination?" The man's laughter was like an accelerant on the hot angry embers burning in the pit of her stomach. She could feel the heat climb up her neck and settle in her cheeks as she made her way back to the bar where he was seated.

"Honey, let me give you a tip," he said. "Grow your hair longer. A man likes to have something to hold onto when he's riding—"

Before she knew what she was doing, she had his shirt collar pulled so tightly that the fat of his neck poured over the cotton tourniquet like a mushroom cap—his face a bright shade of crimson. "Want to finish?" she growled through clenched teeth. He shook his head. When she released him, he crumpled onto the bar like a deflating balloon.

"Nigger bitch," he mumbled between breaths.

"Best be on your way now." Desi's Creole twang rang out from behind her.

The drunk's glossy eyes rolled over the baseball bat threateningly wedged between Desi's elbow and hip and then continued up his six-foot-four-inch frame.

"Fuck this place," the drunk said, elbowing the man next to him. He stood so quickly that his bar stool fell backward.

When the man and his companion were gone, Desi turned concerned eyes on Shae. "You okay there, darlin'?"

Desi had been like a father to Shae—more of a father than her real father was, at least since that day a couple months before his death when he had walked in on her and Jill in the barn. The look on his face could have curdled milk.

"Dad, it's not...I mean...We're..." she had said, as she struggled to cover herself and Jill with what little clothing was within arm's reach.

He didn't have to say anything. His expression said it all. Shame. Revulsion. He stood stock still—the only movement a muscle in his jaw, tightening, releasing, and tightening again. And then, without a word, he just turned and walked off. She'd felt each step heavy in her heart ever since.

As she studied Desi now—his full head of curly dark locks just beginning to gray at his temples, his Pablo Escobar mustache, and his large doe-like deep brown eyes—she felt overcome with gratitude and with love. "Thank you, Desi."

"Seemed to me you already had him crapping his pants. I didn't really do nothing." Desi set the bat in its normal resting place between the register and the shelving unit.

"Thanks just the same." She returned her attention to her normal chores of unloading the dish racks and seeing to her patrons until she heard the door chimes jingle. She grabbed a couple menus and trotted off to greet the customers.

She saw it as soon as she rounded the corner—a large rebel flag centered on the front of his white T-shirt. Around the flag bordered the words: *If this shirt offends you, you need a history lesson.* She ground her teeth. *Marshall Deats.* There were few people Shae hated. Marshall Deats was one of them.

He wasn't looking at her, too busy knocking the caked mud and dirt off his work boots in the doorway. Wet clumps fell onto the welcome mat, obscuring the "H" and "o" in *Home Sweet Home*.

"Marshall," she said in a voice as flat as Florida.

He glanced up. His eyes narrowed and his nostrils flared out like a bull in front of the matador's cape. He grunted and turned away. The product in his hair, which was the color of brown shoe polish, prevented his bangs from following the movement. Thick strands clung to his forehead like those Wacky WallWalkers she used to play with when she was a kid. She had the urge to reach out and grab one with her fingers. Was it solid like matted straw or greasy like coconut oil?

"Get Desi," he demanded to the wall instead of to her.

"So nice talking to you, too," she said, deciding on greasy given the oily shine along his hairline.

She and Marshall had attended the same schools from elementary to high, which meant she knew him before *it* happened. His father had owned Deats Meats, a butcher shop at the center of town. The family was fairly well to do, owning a ranch house on a large plot of land just outside New Orleans. Marshall was an okay kid then, the kind who didn't stand out at much of anything—academics, sports, or girls. He was the kid who never scored the most baskets but never scored the least either. In fact, if it weren't for the yearbook photo, most would have forgotten that he was ever on the team. But the Marshall that emerged from the incident was as obtrusive and offensive as the old one was unassuming.

It happened on a late August day so hot that steam rose off the asphalt. Shae remembered slipping some ice chips into her socks that morning to keep her feet cool. By the time the first bell rung, it had all melted and her soggy socks made a squishing sound when she walked. To compensate for the broken air conditioning, the teachers had propped the doors open with folding chairs and positioned fans in the hallway corners. Shae remembered flyers for organizations and student elections fluttering from the corkboards like streamers. Besides the heat, everything was as normal as the day before—cardboard pizza squares for lunch, a geography test on Southeast Asia's oil production, and a pep rally.

The final bell had just rung and she and the other students were mulling about waiting for the buses or their rides. Shae was sitting in her friend Marissa's idling Yaris in a line of cars packed full of irritated teenagers, trying to feel what relief they could from the cool air streaming through the cars' vents. That was when they heard the sirens.

"What's that?" Marissa asked, rolling down the driver's side window.

Shae shrugged. "Probably an accident."

They watched four police cars, an ambulance, and a fire truck race past the school parking lot.

"If it's an accident," Marissa said, "it's a really big one!"

The following day they learned the cause. And there was nothing accidental about it.

The Monday before, Marshall's sister Mandy Deats, one year behind Shae in school, had shown up with fist-size bruises and an eye blacker than pitch. There were rumors that her asshole boyfriend, Garrett White, had slapped her around. Everyone knew he was a hothead. He'd broken a kid's nose once for just asking what he got on an algebra test. But, to everyone's surprise, Mandy said Tyrell Lewis had attacked her after she rebuffed his advances. Tyrell was a soft-spoken black boy in Shae's homeroom. She'd once seen him carefully cradle a spider that he'd rescued from his locker. Instead of squishing the thing or amputating its legs like the other boys did, Tyrell walked it outside and set it down gently on a patch of grass in the sun.

Regardless of the boy's demeanor, Marshall's father and some of his white trash friends, who had the collective IQ of ketchup, decided to offer Tyrell Lewis what they called, "some good old vigilante justice" but what Shae called, "beating the shit out of him." They hog-tied Tyrell in the backroom of the butcher shop and each of them took turns kicking and swinging at him until he was a bloody and quivering mess. After poor Tyrell finally passed out from all the justice being slung his way, the good old boys treated their sore knuckles to some celebratory cold beers in the kitchen. And that's when Mandy found him. The story went that she untied him, and he ran into the woods, which was pretty amazing given the fact that he had several fractured ribs, swollen-shut eyes, and a ruptured liver. He was taken to the hospital by a farmer who almost hit him with his truck.

Tyrell died in surgery early the next morning. The parish community was rocked by his death. School counselors, who, prior to Tyrell's murder, did little more than talk to the parents of recalcitrant kids, were busy leading remembrance events, memorial services, and grief counseling sessions every day for months. And then when the trial started, the caravan of reporters rolled into town like imperialists—clogging up the streets and filling every diner booth and barstool in a fifteen-mile radius. The local hangouts, including the Hole in the Wall, were so overtaken that the regulars had to travel twenty minutes by car just to get a cup of coffee. Shae remembered that after the incident, her parents wouldn't let her walk the streets alone, fearing—and rightly so—that news of the beating might ignite the town's up-to-then relatively dormant bigotry, and cause what her mother described as, "other crazies dusting off their white robes and sharpening their pitchforks."

Shae couldn't blame her parents for taking precautions. The parish wasn't the most progressive place in the country. In fact, it was right up there with Mobile, Alabama, home of the last recorded lynching in US history in 1981—a lynching that occurred on Shae's birthday—March 21st. She was sure that meant something, but what, she didn't know. The two KKK members responsible for Michael Donald's death were convicted of murder; one was executed and the other was sentenced to life in prison. Not so for Mr. Deats.

Mr. Deats pleaded guilty to the lesser charge of manslaughter, but given the media attention, he was sentenced to the maximum manslaughter charge in the state: forty years. The Deats family lost everything—the business, the house, the town's respect, even each other. Marshall turned hard after that. Even the air around him tasted sour with anger and resentment.

Since high school, he had multiple run-ins with the law, mostly minor drug possessions and petty theft, although he was charged with animal cruelty once when a neighbor saw him punching a dog several times.

Marshall Deats was the Hole in the Wall's gator meat supplier and brought a cooler of fillets every Thursday night like clockwork. To save Shae from the icy exchanges and the wardrobe of racist epithets, Desi did his best to schedule her around his visits but occasionally it couldn't be avoided. *Like now.*

Marshall's demeanor completely transformed from prick to nice guy as Desi approached him. Soon the sounds of them chumming it up had her feeling sick to her stomach.

"How can you be friends with that guy?" she asked Desi as she helped him pack the gator meat into the cooler after Marshall had left.

"Friends?" he laughed. "Give me a little credit, will ya? The guy's a racist pig. A stupid racist, given that he apparently thinks I'm a *gringo*, but regardless, he's the only guy in a twenty-mile radius who hunts and skins gators." As a second-generation Brazilian-American, Desi liked to describe himself as *piel morena*, brown-skinned, despite his light complexion and his obvious ability to pass.

"If it were me, I'd take gator bites off the menu to keep that slime ball out of my restaurant."

"He's here for all of a minute. And it's my *abuela's* recipe."

"A minute too long." Shae pulled the cooler door closed behind them and headed for the bar.

She was busy changing out the register tape when she heard Desi whisper, "The view is so much better, no?"

She followed his eyes to the barstool where the obnoxious drunk from earlier had been sitting.

"Fern!"

"Dart face and all." Fern smiled, her grin so wide that it seemed to reach across the bar and electrify Shae's skin.

"Well, don't hold me in suspense. Who is this *bella dama*?" Desi asked from behind her.

"Fern and I used to be best friends before she up and left me for the Big Apple."

"Well," he said, stepping forward with a hand extended. "Any friend of Shae's is a friend of mine. I'm Desi."

Fern took his hand. "Nice to meet you, Desi."

"Well, don't just stand there, Shae. Get this gal a plate of our signature gator bites. On the house, of course."

"Sure, okay," Shae said and headed for the kitchen. Comping an appetizer was out of character for Desi. He'd only yesterday asked if she could start reusing the coffee pouches. "It's just the drunks who order coffee in a bar," he'd said. "And they're not gonna notice if it ain't Starbucks strong." Maybe he sensed how she felt about Fern. Too bad Fern was straight, she thought for the hundredth time that day. *Let's just hope he doesn't try to play matchmaker.*

Shae prepared the gator bites as fast as she could. She wanted to get back to Fern. She wanted to know what they were talking about. *Please, let it not be about me being gay.*

He had Fern laughing so hard that her head was thrown back and her eyes squinted into almost completely flat lines. It was such a beautiful unrestrained laugh that it made Shae feel almost giddy with happiness. She wished she had been the cause of it, but then maybe she was. Maybe he was spilling all of her embarrassing stories. Her heart raced at the thought.

When she finished with the fryer and set the timer for four minutes, she cleaned up her mess and washed her hands in the metal sink, annoyed that the sound of the water obscured what little bits of their conversation she could hear. She was so absorbed in the Desi and Fern show playing on the mirror behind the bar, that the ding of the timer made her jump. It also apparently made Fern look up, and when she did, their eyes locked. Fire ripped through Shae's body and settled in her cheeks. Fern smiled. Shae immediately looked away and busied herself with the task of plating the fried nuggets.

"So, I was just telling Fern here about that time you and me went fishing and we hooked that large-mouth bass. *El pez mas grande!*"

"Oh god, here we go," Shae said, rolling her eyes. She set the plate in front of Fern.

"You bawled so much that I had to throw the darn thing back. And it was the last I needed for the—"

"Bass Slam Certificate," Shae said. "*I know.*"

"You still owe me for that one, *nina*! Don't think I forgot."

"I don't. Trust me." She winked at Fern.

Fern dipped a fried gator bite into the cup of honey mustard and popped it into her mouth. She moaned as she chewed. The sound made Shae's stomach tighten.

"See!" Desi said. "I told you you'd like it. It's the buttermilk."

The chatter that surrounded them suddenly grew several decibels higher. Shae followed the direction of the patrons' gazes and pointed fingers to the little corner television she'd convinced Desi to have installed before the start of football season.

"The disappearance of a nine-year-old girl has Algiers Point residents on edge, and rightly so," the newscaster said. She was standing in front of the Algiers courthouse. "Alia Ambrois seemed to vanish into thin air after being dropped off by a Martin Behrman Elementary School bus last Tuesday, less than half a block from her home on Olivier Street. In the nine days since, there have been no sightings of Alia."

A uniformed police officer filled the screen. The caption read *Algiers Police Detective Dan Fowler.* "We're interviewing Alia's school friends and reviewing social media channels," he said, "but we don't have a lot of information to go on from this starting point."

The newscaster's voice returned. "Alia Ambrois is African American, four-foot-four and approximately sixty pounds. She was last seen wearing a pink dress, her hair fashioned in pigtails." The screen filled with an image of the girl.

The same girl Shae had seen in the water. The same girl she had been in her dream. Suddenly the world was spinning. And then everything went dark.

CHAPTER THREE

With a start, Shae awoke. Her heart racing. Her breathing rapid. She opened her eyes to a graffitied wall that pronounced *B.C. hearts P.B.* in a colorful bubble letter street style that overlapped *Jenna's a slut* in clashing fat capitals. By the looks of it, she was in some sort of shack that moonlighted as a local teen hangout. The wood floor was anemic-looking, like a weathered deck or an old park picnic table that had survived a century of rainy seasons—littered with beer bottles, a tackle box, and some empty gas cans.

The walls, in contrast, were alive like skin. The peeling gray paint had obviously been flaking off for some time given the dandruff of sludge colored chips decorating the floor's perimeter. Rusty stains branched throughout the walls like the bare tree limbs of childhood nightmares or a desert's veiny rivers from an aerial view. The narrow copper tendrils bled into the surrounding paint like an infection.

A stinging sensation drew her attention to her knees. Ground dirt and dried blood clung to her like the gunk on the bottom of a casserole dish. But that wasn't what caught her breath. Her knees had apparently shrunk to half their size. Either that or they weren't her knees at all. She reached a hand up to her hair. *Please don't let it be.* On one side her hair was matted and on the other it was banded together in a ponytail with a beaded holder. Alia Ambrois. Fear seized her stomach and set her heart into a frenzied rhythm. The man. The dogs. She ran for the door. The knob wouldn't turn. She slammed it with her shoulder. Even with all of her strength, it wouldn't budge. She needed another way out.

There was no furniture except for a stained twin mattress worthy of a horror movie. Some wires stretched loosely across the wooden planks in the ceiling from a wall outlet to a solitary light fixture sans bulb in the center. The only light came from two rectangular wood windows in the walls adjacent to the door—the kind that pushed out rather than up. These, though, wouldn't push at all. A thick film of grime covered the glass and muted the sunlight. There in the upper right corner of one of the windows was a clearing, barely larger than a palm print. Through it Shae could see blue sky. Somehow she knew that Alia had stared at that swath of sky, too, combing through her thoughts for all of the things she could remember that had that same blue. The blue of her brother's bike, the blue of the bathroom walls at school, the blue of her Pony Bright doll, the blue of the big globe in her father's office, the blue of her princess doll's dress. But the memories of the things she *wanted* to forget but couldn't were too much with her. The memory of the man—the Saints ball cap man, pushing a coffee tin into her hands. "To piss in," he'd said, his voice muffled by the handkerchief around his mouth and nose. Shae remembered. Only they weren't her memories. They were Alia's.

At night when the temperature dropped, Alia had propped her knees beneath the fabric of her dress and wrapped her arms around herself to keep warm. And she'd listened in the dark. She'd listened and she'd waited. When he was there, she mapped his movements by the sounds of crunching leaves and grass outside the shack. Always on guard. Afraid to close her eyes even for a moment, squeezing an old rusty fork she'd found in the tackle box so hard between her fingers that they were bloodless. When she'd pry them open in the morning, they'd ache from the strain. Shae could feel it, too, as she stretched her fingers to their full length—a stubborn resistance, a dull pain, a warning.

Something cold splashed onto Shae's face, making her gasp. "What the?" She looked up to find Fern staring back at her, Fern's bottom lip wedged between her teeth, her eyes wide and reflective.

"You okay?"

Shae squeezed her eyes shut and opened them again, half expecting to return to the shack. But Fern was still there. And so was the Hole in the Wall. *It was a dream. Just a dream.*

Fern's fingers caressed her cheek as if she were a small child. She resisted the urge to lean into the touch.

"Take it easy." Desi's square chin and big brown eyes came into view. "You had a spill."

"A spill?"

"You fainted," he explained. "I told you to have your blood checked. How many times do I have to tell you to take care of yourself? You can't live on plants alone."

Her scattered thoughts were slow to congeal. When they did, they zeroed in on one solitary fact with laser-like focus—her head in Fern's lap. Fern's thighs. *Her head was sandwiched between Fern's thighs!* The thought was enough to raise her temperature so quickly and with such force that she imagined the mercury in her internal thermometer ringing a bell like the one in that high striker game at the county fair, the one with the mallet. She recognized it immediately—arousal. *Fuck.* She struggled to push herself upright with her elbows but was stopped by a palm on her shoulder.

"Lie still. Just until you get your bearings," Desi said. "You fell pretty hard."

Her skin was cold. She shivered. The fabric of her T- shirt was dark and wet, and the combination of the dampness, the cool air-conditioned air, and her aroused state had her nipples standing at attention like good little soldiers. She reached an arm across herself to hide them from view.

"Did you hurt your arm in the fall?" Fern asked.

"What?" As she struggled to right herself, she caught a whiff of alcohol powerful enough to necessitate taxi rides home for everyone in the vicinity. The rank smell was, apparently, coming from her. "Why do I smell like a brewery?"

"You fainted," Desi explained. "I splashed you awake…like in the movies. All that I had at the time was…Guinness." He mumbled and squinted his eyes as if she were going to take a swing at him.

"Jeez, Dez!" She would've swung at him if she wasn't trying to keep her nipples from poking Fern's eyes out.

"Seriously, are you okay?" Fern asked, taking the temperature of her forehead with the back of her hand. "Are you sick?"

"I'm fine. I'm not—"

"She's anemic," he interrupted. "Needs to eat meat. Not that quinoa and kale crap she's always trying to get me to taste." He made a face.

"*Was* anemic. I've felt fine lately. I just…" *Just what? Dreamed for the second time that I was a missing elementary schoolgirl? Teleported to an old shack somewhere?*

"Just?" Fern prompted, her brows scrunching together over the bridge of her nose.

There was a genuine concern in her expression that made Shae want to explain it all—the shack, the coffee can, the peeling paint, the solitary pigtail holder. But none of it would make any sense. She would sound crazy for sure. "I guess… I guess I was tired is all."

Desi frowned. "People don't pass out because they're tired, Shae. Promise me you'll go to the doctor and have your blood work done again."

She blew out a frustrated breath. "I don't need—"

"*Please*, Shae?" Fern asked.

She opened her mouth to protest but no sound came out. She felt incapable of saying no to those pretty eyes as blue as the sky and those plump kissable lips, lips from which she couldn't detach her gaze at the moment. "Okay, I promise."

Desi hooked his hands under her arms and pulled her to a seated position. "Are you dizzy?"

Shae could feel everyone's eyes on her, including the customers at the bar and in the booths. She would have given anything to disappear. "No, I'm fine. *Really*. I feel fine." She made a half-hearted attempt to fix her beer-soaked clothes. The stench nauseated her. "I obviously need to head home for a change of clothes."

"You need to *stay* home and rest," Desi said.

Shae frowned. She couldn't afford to lose the hours.

"Don't worry," he said, reading her mind. "I'll pay you for the full shift."

While it was true that she needed the money, she was embarrassed that he'd said it in front of Fern. The previous spring was the first harvest without her father and the first collection notice, too. Shae's father had paid for equipment and feed with a crop lien. That wasn't all that unusual. Crop liens could work to the farmer's benefit if the harvest's value turned out to be greater than what was anticipated. It had taken time, though, after his death, for Shae and her mother to get the farm back and running again. The harvest had suffered as a result. And because of that lien, they were still in the red two years later. They didn't seem to be making any headway, either, despite Shae's income at the bar and both her and her mother's tireless hours in the fields. With the interest compounding faster than the harvest cycle, Shae worried they were fighting a losing battle.

She glanced nervously at Fern, hoping she'd missed the comment. The sympathy that softened her eyes said that she hadn't. Shae didn't want to be pitied, especially by Fern. What she wanted was to get the hell out of there. She angrily fished her keys out of the back pocket of her jeans.

"You're not driving on the scooter after fainting like that," Desi said.

"I said I'm fine."

"And if you get pulled over, how are you going to explain your eau de hops?" he laughed.

"Water, Dez," Shae grumbled. "Most people use water."

"Just wait, I'll drive you home." He pulled the wall phone off its cradle. "Let me call Will to cover for me while I—"

Fern stood. "I'll take you."

The next thing Shae knew, she was sitting in the passenger seat of Ruby Beaumont's Prius, desperately trying not to melt to ash as Fern reached across her to fasten her seatbelt and accidentally brushed her hand against Shae's right breast. Normally, she'd refuse such help. She could put her own damn seatbelt on. But feeling Fern reach across her like that made her forget her bravado, her independence. And she just wanted more of whatever Fern was offering. More of Fern, in fact.

"Good?" Fern asked, latching the buckle.

Unable to speak, Shae nodded.

"So, do you still live with your parents?"

Shae ground her teeth and turned toward the window. *And here it is. She thinks I'm pathetic. And why wouldn't she? Twenty years old and still living with mom, waitressing at some backwoods bar, no education, no prospects, no future.* "I'm gonna get my own place," she said. "I've been saving money and—" She felt a hand close on her shoulder.

"I'm not judging. I just want to know where I'm taking you."

The touch, however brief, was enough to make the anger disappear. "I live with Mom," she admitted.

"Are your parents divorced?"

"No." She took a deep breath and exhaled through her nostrils, her way of cooling the pain that pulsed in her throat every time she had to say it. "Dad died two years ago."

"Oh my god. I'm so sorry."

Shae closed her eyes and saw her father's scowl that day in the barn. "We weren't close the last few months." She tried to swallow past the lump forming in her throat.

"Why not? I mean, you always seemed really tight."

They had been tight, tighter than tight. She had emulated her father. When she was little, she would slip her tiny feet into his giant work boots and clomp around the house in them until the noise would wear down her mother's patience. She'd follow him around like a puppy, imitating his every movement. She'd often be seen with a sugarcane stalk wedged in her cheek, spitting its juices on the ground like her father did with his tobacco.

"Listen," she said, blinking back tears at the memory. "If it's all right with you. I'd rather not talk about it."

"Oh, of course. I'm sorry." Fern looked embarrassed. Shae hoped it wasn't embarrassment for her. Not only did she live with her mother and work at a crappy hole-in-the-wall place, but she was also now a blubbering mess.

She dropped her gaze to the floorboards, wishing she could be anywhere but there with Fern. "Do you remember where the farm is?"

Fern turned the key and the engine came to life. "Do I remember?" she asked, aghast. "Do you know how many bike tire treads I wore down between my house and yours?" She glanced in the rearview mirror and pushed the gear into place. "I could probably get there blindfolded." She gave Shae's thigh a quick squeeze. "I'll have you there faster than you can say Jack Robinson."

Shae couldn't help but smile. Ruby had often used that phrase to describe the girls' quickness—flitting here and there "like gnats," she'd said. "As soon as you arrive, you're leaving again, faster than you can say Jack Robinson."

Shae was surprised by how easily that little memory had jolted her out of her sadness like a springboard, and how Fern had known exactly what to say and do to make her feel better. After ten years. It was like the ten years had somehow fallen away and here they were again, two nine-year-old best friends.

"What?" Fern was studying her, the quizzical look on her face making Shae wonder what hers may have revealed.

"Nothing, I just like having you around is all."

Fern smiled.

They settled into a comfortable silence, the sound of the engine alleviating the need to talk. The lulling movement of the car got the better of Shae's exhaustion and she leaned back against the headrest and closed her eyes. Behind her lids was a cascade of the day's events—the nightmarish dream of being chased through the swamplands and the other dream of being imprisoned in that shack. It had to be a coincidence, she thought. She must've heard the story somewhere. Maybe her mother had the news on while she was falling asleep and Shae's sleeping brain wove the details of the story into her subconscious. Or maybe seeing the real Alia on the television at the bar colored her memory of the girl in her dream and made it seem like it was her when it really wasn't.

Hell, maybe Desi was right and she was low on iron. Whatever it was, she hoped it would stop.

As if she didn't have enough stress with keeping the farm afloat and dealing with weird dreams she couldn't make sense of, there was Fern—coming back into her life after being so long absent and throwing her emotions into a tailspin. All those years of hanging on every mention of her name, and all the time pretending not to care. The exhaustion of pretending was something familiar to her. She was out to family and her friends, but to everyone else, she just didn't talk about her sexuality. Not that she switched her pronouns—that was far too dishonest for her—but she did stay silent and occasionally fibbed just a little to protect herself.

Last week, for example, Ruby caught Shae in the act of ogling the photos of Fern attached to Ruby's refrigerator. "I thought I saw some condensation on the back panel," she'd choked. "So, I was just checking if you had a Freon leak or something."

She forced her mouth shut, thinking she'd give herself away by overexplaining. Ruby had just smiled that annoyingly knowing smile of hers and turned back to kneading the dough with her flour-covered fists. There was something about Ruby. It was there in the way she held her head just slightly to the left side, her eyes in a partial squint. It was as if she existed in a perpetual state of considering things. And maybe she did know about Shae's sexuality. Maybe she even knew about Shae's crush on Fern. But if she did, she never brought it up. She must also have known Shae wasn't prepared for that conversation. In some ways Shae wasn't prepared to acknowledge her feelings at all. Pining for a straight girl. She'd had enough straight-girl heartbreak to know how this kind of thing ended, and yet she just couldn't stop herself.

Even if Ruby didn't have some special kind of wisdom superpower, she could probably guess that Shae was gay. It wasn't hard to tell. Aside from a brief stint in middle school when she let "Night brace Jeffrey" feel her up behind the bleachers at a football game, Shae had only dated girls. And she wasn't the most feminine girl in town with her very short hair and her aversion to makeup, jewelry, and anything pink. Not that she was butch. She liked to think of herself as a tomboy. On a good day she could pass for an androgynous Alicia Keys.

"Are you sleeping?"

The question sounded just as it had all those years ago on the many nights Shae had slept over at Fern's house. It was a question that was usually followed by a nudge with a knee or a poke with a finger. If she wasn't already awake, she definitely would be then. The memory lifted her lips into a smile, despite herself.

"No," she said. "I'm up."

"You know, I…" Fern started and then stopped. With her gaze on the windshield, Shae was free to study her profile, the delicate slope of her nose, the curve of her chin, the arc of shadow that stretched across her neck to her earlobe like a sliver of moon.

"You what?" she asked.

"I… I meant to write," Fern continued. "I mean I did write."

"What?"

"I started letters but never finished them."

"You wrote to me?"

"It just wasn't the same—you know, writing and talking to you—the real you, I mean." Fern glanced at Shae. It was a quick glance, so quick that Shae wasn't entirely sure if it really happened or if she'd just imagined it. "I've never had a friend like that—like you, I mean—since then."

"Well, for what it's worth," Fern said, maneuvering the car into Shae's driveway, "I'm sorry I didn't write."

"Don't worry about it," Shae said nonchalantly, as if it had never bothered her, as if she'd never even thought about it, as if she wasn't on cloud nine right now. "It doesn't matter."

Fern shifted the car into park and faced her. "It does matter," she said. "And I'm sorry."

Despite her feigned bravado, tears pricked at Shae's eyes. "Okay," she managed.

"So, what're we doing tomorrow?"

Shae laughed. Without thinking, she pulled Fern into a hug. "I'm glad you're home."

"I feel like I'm home," Fern said. "For the first time in a long time."

CHAPTER FOUR

Fern was stretched across her bed on her stomach, her arms propped up on bent elbows, her chin resting in her palms, and her feet moving to the beat of the music pulsing through her earbuds. She was staring at her open Aquatic Entomology textbook—the class she was taking at the community college— and rereading the first paragraph of chapter one for the fifth time. She was trying to pay attention, but she kept drifting back to the conversation she had with Desi at the bar.

She just couldn't believe it. If anyone would've known, it would be her. She and Shae had slept together more times than either had slept alone, and they shared all manner of secrets— things that even now embarrassed her. She had memories of racing Shae to the river after the final school bell. Anxious to feel the cool water on their sunbaked skin, they'd shed their clothes as they went. She'd swum naked with a *lesbian*! Even though she had nodded right through Desi's revelation, voiced the obligatory expressions of agreement, "Of course, yeah, right," it had hit her like a ton of bricks, practically knocked the wind right out of her. *Shae is gay? Shae dates women?*

"So, the last girl she dated was a real winner," Desi had said. "Straight, married preacher's daughter. Can you believe it? A freakin' preacher's daughter? Girl, you can't get any more cliché than that!" His voice had taken on a flamboyant, effeminate lilt with the "girl" exclamation.

A married woman? Not Shae. It just didn't fit with the girl Fern had known. Shae was as honest and as moral as they came. They were seven or maybe eight when they'd accidentally thrown a softball through the Petersons' garage door window. As soon as Fern saw the garage lights come on, she took off like a bat of out hell, running so fast that it took her a few seconds to realize Shae wasn't at her side. She turned back to find that Shae was already making her way up the Petersons' brick driveway. Shae got grounded for a week because of the window, and Fern? There was no sense in both of them getting in trouble.

And now, honest Shae is out seducing married women—a preacher's daughter, no less. The thought piqued Fern's interest as if it were taboo like the stash of *Maxim* magazines she'd found in her friend John's closet when she was fourteen.

As she'd listened to Desi tell the story of Shae's love life, the buzzer had drawn her attention to the kitchen, the entrance of which was reflected in the mirror behind the bar. When she looked up, she found a pair of brown eyes the color of melted chocolate fixed on her. She would've looked away, but she didn't have to because Shae did it first—turned her whole head, in fact, so that Fern was left studying her profile.

Fern didn't know what had possessed her to volunteer to give Shae a ride. The offer had bubbled up inside her and erupted from her mouth before she had even a moment to think about it. Of course she'd known lesbians. It wasn't like she lived under a rock. Lesbians were practically ubiquitous at the university— in her classes, in her dorm. And Katy Perry's "I Kissed a Girl" played on an almost permanent loop at university keg parties. But she'd never really *known* any lesbians.

There were so many questions she wanted to ask Shae. *When did you know? Who did you come out to first?* More importantly, she wanted to ask, *What's it like with a girl?* and *Who makes the first move?* But it's not like she could weave those questions into the conversation in a way that would seem natural. And she shouldn't be asking them anyway. She didn't know Shae well enough, but it didn't matter because Shae was clearly too tired.

So instead of asking her questions, she studied her. Shae was fit, athletic-looking, as if she were one of those rare people who actually used their gym memberships past February. Lesbians probably found her sexy, Fern thought as she studied the musculature of Shae's upper arms and shoulders. And that cocoa skin tone, of which Fern, with her prone-to-sunburn Casper complexion, had forever been jealous, was downright creamy. Pretty wasn't the right word. Shae was more handsome than pretty, but handsome was too manly a term. She was androgynous and sexy—like a jungle cat—cautious, sleek, and strong.

Shae had surprised her with the hug. When they were young, they'd hugged all the time—hello, goodbye, even just because. But knowing that she was a lesbian made the hug feel different. It was like those pictures that had images hidden inside them— the bear in the mountains or the lion in the jungle. It took a while to find the camouflaged image, but once you did, you couldn't un-see it. The original picture was forever altered.

The knowing was like that for Fern. Now that she knew Shae was a lesbian, every interaction between them, even the hug, was colored by it. So when Shae's arms circled her middle and the feeling of Shae's breasts pressing against her own drifted into her consciousness, she felt unusually warm and had to fight the urge to move closer still. And now she wasn't sure what to do with that feeling or what it meant.

"I'm glad you're home," Shae said. The warm breath expelled with the words made the hair on Fern's neck stand on end.

It was just some healthy curiosity, she thought. *I'm definitely not a lesbian.*

She turned her attention back to the excerpt that started the textbook chapter: a Hungarian folksong that likened love to the short life of the adult riverine mayfly—a romance that ends before it even begins to bloom.

* * *

"What do you mean she knows?" Shae's fingers closed so tightly around the glass that even she was surprised it didn't shatter into pieces.

Desi pinched his right brow between his index finger and thumb as if doing so would tame the wild white hairs that jutted out of the black thicket like porcupine quills. This was his "I'm thinking" pose, which he donned when he wasn't sure of what to say or do next. He'd done it so many times while they played chess that Shae actually rushed toward checkmate for fear that he'd wear a bald spot right into his brow's center.

"I mean," he said, releasing his hostage brow, "I didn't know it was some kind of secret. When did you decide to go back in the closet anyway?"

"I didn't." Shae set the glass down on the counter harder than she intended, causing some of the empty beer bottles nearby to clatter together as if in conversation. "I just…I didn't want her to know."

"Is she a homophobe? She didn't even bat an eye when I mentioned your ex, the preacher's daughter."

"You told her about Cheryl?" Shae was mortified. *Great! Now, I'm not only a sexual deviant but I'm a homewrecker too.*

He inspected a glass for water stains in the light of the Budweiser lamp overhead. "Shae, darling, lest you forget, you are not the kind of girl who cares what other people think." He heated the glass with his breath and used a towel to polish it. "Unless…" he said, lifting his left eyebrow into a dramatic arc on his forehead, "…you like her."

"I don't," Shae snapped, a little too quickly to be believed. She turned her attention to readying the next rack for the dishwasher.

"Mmm." He was clearly unconvinced.

"I like her, but I don't *like* her."

"Whatever you say."

"I don't!"

"Methinks the lady doth protest too much."

"I'm not! I mean, I don't."

He slid the glass on the shelf and turned to face Shae. "This is me you're talking to, girlie. You forget. I *know* you. I've seen you at your lowest—after Cheryl went back to her husband, Mr. Muscle Milk. If I recall, I found you shoveling salted caramel Häagen Dazs in your mouth and washing it down with box o' cabernet."

Shae shivered with revulsion.

"But you survived, mostly because I managed to wrestle the wine IV out of your veins and took you to Strands for that new do."

Shae couldn't help but laugh at the memory of the layered razor cut with which she had left the salon. The style was so ultra-feminine that she looked like she was in drag. Despite it being the worst hairstyle she'd ever had, it took her from moping around the house and feeling sorry for herself to laughing so hard, that by the next morning she could barely work her ab muscles enough to pull herself out of bed.

Desi did know her. He could read her better than she could read herself. "Maybe I like her a little," she conceded.

"A little my ass."

"Little and your ass should never be in the same sentence."

He threw a dishtowel at her and it hit her square in the chest before it fell to the floor in a crumpled ball. She kicked it with the toe of her boot.

"I don't really know her," Shae admitted. "I mean we haven't seen each other in ten years. And she's straight."

"Honey, we were all straight before we weren't."

Shae laughed. "Even if she weren't straight, which she is, she's way out of my league."

"There aren't any leagues. And don't sell yourself short. You're a catch, almost Bass Slam Certificate worthy," he said and winked.

Some loud voices brought Shae's attention back to the bar. A group of guys, not much older than she, had just entered and were now milling about finding stools. Judging by their matching camo gear and rubber boots, it was a hunting party.

One of the boys bent down to read the names on the beer tap handles, giving her a glimpse of the boy behind him, his greasy head of hair the color of shoe polish. Her heart sank when she recognized Marshall Deats. Given Desi's heavy sigh, he must've seen him too. "Your shift's almost over," he said. "If you want to get out of here, it's okay with me."

There were five besides Marshall, mostly clean cut, jock types. She recognized one from high school—Danny Fowler— two years her senior and captain of the wrestling team.

Marshall glanced in her direction then sneered and looked away. She took a deep breath and exhaled noisily through her nostrils. "He's not going to chase me out of here," she said.

"Suit yourself." Desi shrugged and turned his attention back to the tray of glassware he'd been working on before the interruption.

"What can I get you boys?" Shae asked the tall one with the overbite. A handsome dark-haired guy quickly elbowed his way to the front and slapped a hundred-dollar bill on the counter. "A bucket of your best on ice," he said. "And keep the change."

Something about him was familiar, but not from school or town. It was a more distant familiarity, as if she'd seen him in a magazine or on television.

"Quit showing off, Copeland!" one of them said.

Copeland. Where had she heard that name?

The boy named Copeland stood and addressed the one who had just spoken. When he did, Shae saw something gold poking out of the back pocket of his pants. It was the bill of a baseball hat, curled like a rolled magazine. Barely visible, on the hat's crushed black crown, was the raised embroidered fleur de lis. She felt the hair on her arms stand on end. *It couldn't be.*

"You better watch it, Copeland. She's checking out your ass," one of them said and laughed.

Shae ignored him and turned to the ice chest. In the mirror behind the bar, Copeland's gaze was fixed on her. Brown eyes—just like the Saints ball cap man.

She steadied her breathing and forced herself to scoop ice into the bucket. There were plenty of Saints fans with brown eyes, she reasoned. And she hadn't gotten a good enough look at the guy to recall his features with any kind of certainty, especially with the handkerchief obscuring much of his face. Besides, it was just a crazy dream.

Later that evening, Shae was lounging around the kitchen while her mother, Camilla, made dinner.

"So what's this I hear about you passing out at work yesterday?" Camilla used the side of her kitchen knife to scrape the remaining bits of herbs into the pan.

"Did you know that cilantro hatred is genetic?" Shae asked as she reached in to spear a zucchini wedge, her fork's destination blocked by her mother's wooden spoon.

"Our family must've been playing hooky the day that gene was dispensed."

Shae smiled. "No one says 'hooky' anymore." She pulled her phone from her back pocket and began typing.

"Are you going to tell me what happened? Were you tired? Did you feel sick?"

"The Americanism 'play hooky' most likely came from *hoekje*, a Dutch name for a game of hide and seek originating in the late eighteen forties. There's also a theory that it came from the nineteenth century colloquial phrase 'hooky-crooky,' suggesting something dishonest."

"You're being hooky-crooky right now by avoiding my questions."

Shae snapped her phone closed. "Desi's just squawking. If he didn't gossip, they'd revoke his Priscilla Desert Queen membership."

"It doesn't matter who told me. What matters," she said, pulling Shae's chin toward her with her fingers, "is why my daughter is passing out."

Shae pushed herself up onto the counter with her palms. "I didn't pass out," she said, kicking her feet out like a child. Her mother's eyebrows dipped in disbelief. "I mean, I did pass out," she corrected, "but it wasn't like a medical thing."

"What do you mean?"

"Well, I…" Shae wound a string she'd found hanging from the hem of her sweatshirt around her index finger and watched the now bulging segments go pink. She could hear the edge of nervousness in her mother's voice and knew this was dangerous territory. *Better to just sweep it under the rug.* "Listen, don't worry about it, Mom. It was nothing."

"Shae Noelle Williams!" Her mother rarely used her full name. So when she did, Shae couldn't help but pay attention. The sound of her middle name was so foreign to her ears that its effect was almost Pavlovian, making her whole body turn in the direction from which it was spoken. "Tell me what's going on," her mother demanded.

Shae could see the concern in her eyes, the worry wrinkle forming between her brows. And she knew they'd reached that point when Camilla wouldn't be satisfied with anything less than the truth. "I think…I mean, well, it started with a dream."

"A dream?"

"Yesterday morning when you woke me up, I was having this dream. A nightmare really. I was being chased—only it wasn't really me. I was someone else. A girl."

"With pigtails," her mother added, seeming to connect the dots of that morning's conversation.

Shae nodded. "Then later at the bar, I heard this news report about that missing girl. You know, the one who disappeared on her way home from school."

"The girl from Algiers Point?"

"Yeah." Shae absently picked at the label of an empty can of diced tomatoes. "When I saw her picture…I don't know how… but…"

"But what?" Her mother stopped stirring and faced her.

"It was her," Shae said, "the girl from my dream."

Camilla's eyes widened.

"And that's when I passed out. From shock, I guess." Shae swallowed, wishing the story ended there. "I must've had another dream, because the next thing I knew I was in some kind of shack. Only I wasn't me. I was her again."

"She was right," her mother said, the words muffled by her hand cupping her mouth.

"What? Who?"

"I can't believe she was right," she said.

"Who was right, Mom?"

"Your grandmother."

"Grandma? What does Grandma have to do with anything?"

"She used to say that she could see it in you, like you were ready to take flight, your little toes curling over the edge of some imaginary platform, your knees bent, your whole body wound like a tight coil in a metal spring." Camilla's shock transformed into pensiveness, her index finger tapping out a steady rhythm on her bottom lip. It was the exact same expression she wore when she played Sudoku or studied a complicated recipe.

"Mom, what are you talking about? You're not making any sense."

"You didn't dream that girl, Shae."

"What?"

Camilla paced the room like a robot vacuum cleaner. "One minute Mom would be pulling the pot roast out of the oven," she said, "and the next she'd be passed out on the linoleum."

"What are you talking about?"

"I'd pull her hair, even pry her eyes open with my fingers." She turned to face Shae. "But she wouldn't wake up."

"I don't understand."

"The first time it happened, I thought she was dead. I mean, imagine how scary that is to a five-year-old. They told me she had a condition called narcolepsy that caused sudden bouts of sleep. I was fourteen when I learned the truth. She'd woken up from one of these narcoleptic slumbers in a full panic—gasping for air, clutching her chest. I was playing in the sprinklers when I heard her scream. That night she told me everything."

"She'd jumped for the first time when she was around your age—eighteen I think. She and dad were at the drive-in movie theater. Dad had just returned from the concession stand with some snacks and sodas. And before he'd even handed her the popcorn carton, she was gone. Like that." Camilla snapped her fingers for effect. "The next thing she knew, she was underwater in a scuba suit, with a chorus of beeps and alarms ringing in her ears. And she was running out of air."

"Oh my god! Did the person drown?"

"Before she could find out, she was back in the Chevy, popcorn spilled all over her lap, staring into my father's panicked expression as he fanned her with a box of Raisinets."

"So, she had a dream."

"That's just it, Shae. It *wasn't* a dream."

"I don't understand."

"Your grandmother started to take note of dates, times, and her surroundings during the jumps. She looked in mirrors when she could. And then when she was back, she'd search for the people and stories that fit what she remembered. I spent a lot of my childhood in library basements watching her scroll through microfilm spools of newspaper articles."

"A coincidence then."

"No, Shae. The people, the places, the experiences—they were all real."

"But that's impossible." Shae shook her head as if doing so would erase their conversation like the image on an Etch-A-Sketch.

"Honey, I know it's hard to believe."

"It's not just hard to believe. It's crazy!"

"It may be crazy, but it's true."

"So, what you're saying then is this girl—Alia Ambrois—she's…she's really…?"

"She's really out there."

Shae stared at her mother, wishing that she'd laugh and say that this was all a joke, that she was just kidding. "But what am I supposed to do?"

"You need to remember what you can—the color of the walls, the smell in the air, anything that could help the police zero in on her location or her captor."

"*The police?* What am I supposed to tell them? That I have some kind of new age superhero gene that lets me jump into people's bodies when they're in crisis?"

Camilla studied her daughter. "You tell them whatever you need to get them to listen." She took her daughter's hands in her own. "You have a gift, Shae. And with that gift comes responsibility."

Shae exhaled noisily. "More responsibility, that's exactly what I need."

Camilla frowned. "I know you've had a lot on your plate—what with the farm and…"

"I don't want this."

"I'm afraid it's not a matter of wanting it." Camilla wiped her hands on her apron and set the spoon on the counter next to the stovetop. "Your grandmother left you something," she said. "I'll be right back."

Shae couldn't believe it. None of it made any sense. She halfheartedly pushed the stew around with the spoon. Like little road bumps, the now burnt ends on the bottom of the pan caused her spoon to pause and jump. She imagined judges criticizing the lack of gracefulness in her swirl. *Of all people, why me? And of all the genetic traits to be saddled with—varicose veins, small breasts, bad eyesight, cilantro aversion—why am I stuck with this one?*

Her mother returned with an envelope. Contrary to its yellowed corners and its weathered look, Shae's name was written in the center in her grandmother's careful hand. Shae easily recognized her unusually pronounced slant in the *S* and soft loop in the *h*. "Why didn't you give this to me sooner?"

"She made me swear that I would wait for when…or if…"

Shae ran the pads of her fingers over the envelope as if she could read her grandmother's thoughts in Braille on its surface.

"Go on then," her mother said, "Go on and listen to your grandmother."

Dearest Granddaughter,

Assuming Camilla did as she was told, which, considering her teenage years is questionable at best, the very fact that you're reading this means that my adventure has ended and that yours has just begun. You are no doubt confused, perhaps even frightened. But let me assure you that this change that you are going through is a gift. Truly it is. When you complete your first assignment, you will think so, too. That's what I've come to call them—assignments. When I realized that these jumps weren't haphazard, that they were in fact given to us by something or someone, the title seemed fitting. But perhaps I am getting ahead of myself.

Let's start at the beginning, shall we? We have a unique condition. While it doesn't have a proper name, my great grandmother called it Skinwalking. And there have been several Skinwalkers in our genetic line—interestingly, all women from nonconsecutive generations. This condition allows us to walk in someone else's skin—temporarily until that someone returns to it. While we wear their skin, we feel as if it's our own. We see through their eyes. We hear through their ears. We run with their legs. And we feel their pain, although we are not the ones who suffer the physical effects of that pain. They are. So it is our job to keep their bodies safe from harm. To the best that I can tell, the jumping happens when the person wants desperately to escape a threat of some kind—either something internal like a strangling guilt or something external like a <u>Wizard of Oz</u>-worthy tornado. Most often, though, the threat is other people. It will not be something that you can control, and as far as I can tell, there is no way to expedite your return to your body. It will just happen—both your arrival and your exit. So, you will have to be prepared.

Over the years, I've learned several things that proved essential, some were passed on to me by my grandmother and others I simply learned through trial and error. First, we do feel whatever the body we're in feels and the person to whom the body belongs will have to suffer the consequences of any physical pain endured during our stay. So it's essential that we learn how to keep ourselves and their bodies safe. That means training—and lots of it. Your first step should be to enroll in a self-defense class. And if you're able, learn some more advanced defense techniques, like kickboxing. We women hold much of our strength and our power in our legs. Another aspect of safety is learning basic emergency care techniques—how to stitch a laceration, that sort of thing. At the very least, take a CPR course. And along the same lines, develop some basic wilderness survival skills. You should learn things like how to locate a suitable campsite, how to build a shelter, and how to start a fire with a battery.

Second, know how to ask basic questions and how to call for help in as many languages as you can. I can't tell you how many times I landed in places where I didn't understand a lick of what was being spoken. The language barrier makes completing an assignment almost impossible! Third, start to be mindful of the physical signs of an impending jump. This will afford you what little time you have to prepare—to move things out of the way, for example—so that you don't break your neck on the fall. For me, the signs were a slowing heart rate and the appearance of floaters—tiny circles of light that would flash in my line of vision like little exploding stars or pixie dust.

Finally, you will need help on this journey. You cannot do this alone. You'll need people whom you can trust, people who have skill sets you do not have, both here on this plane and in the spiritual one. Ruby Beaumont knew about our family and about me. She can help you connect with some of the right people.

I know this is a great deal to take in, and perhaps it's nothing that you want. But it is here, nonetheless, and you must make the best of it. This, Shae, is your destiny, as it once was mine. And fulfilling that destiny will make you whole.

All of my love,
Grandma Jo

Shae read and reread the letter, trying to make sense of it. What she remembered most about her grandmother was how strong her hands were. Her grandmother's fingers would wrap around Shae's tiny hands as she guided her spoon through the cookie dough, the brownie mix, or the baking soda paste for a school project. The strength in those fingers struck Shae, even then, as incongruous with her skin, which was wrinkled like crepe paper.

Shae remembered a few times when Josephine had taken her to the dojo. While little Shae perfected the crane kick from the *Karate Kid* movies, her grandmother practiced martial arts moves with people half her age. At the time, she had thought it was exercise, a way for her grandmother to stay healthy. But now that she studied the memory from a more grown up perspective, she realized that her grandmother—her sixty-some-year-old grandmother at the time—was practicing throws, takedowns, chokes, and joint locks. *Jumping into other people's skin? Can it be true? And if it is true, can I save Alia Ambrois?*

CHAPTER FIVE

After dinner, Ruby retired to her studio and Fern stretched out on the sofa in the living room to watch television—well, to listen to television. What she was watching was static and a few shadowy shapes that might resemble people or furniture, she wasn't sure which. Her grandmother's thirteen-inch television was only able to find three snowy stations when she scanned for antenna channels. Her eyelids were just beginning to close when the sound of a scooter brought her attention to the window.

At the sight of Shae in the driveway pushing the kickstand down with the heel of her boot, Fern's heart beat faster. She frowned at her jersey's faded high school lacrosse logo and the baggy gray sweats she was wearing—an outfit not even worthy of a quick tampon run to the convenience store. She cringed at her reflection in the hallway mirror and tried her best to fix her hair. It was no use, though. Finger combing did little to tame its wispy wildness.

Fern opened the door before Shea completed a knock, leaving Shae's fist to hang frozen in the air as if she were mid-chant at a protest rally.

"Hi," Fern said.

"Hi, I'm sorry to bother you, I—"

"Oh you're not bothering me. I'm watching *Wheel of Fortune* in Spanish, bored out of my mind." *Stop talking.* "I mean, do you want to come in?" She held the door open for Shae to pass. "How are you? After the fainting thing yesterday..." *Why was she talking so much?*

"I'm good." Shae was shifting her weight from one foot to the other, making Fern wonder whether she was nervous or waiting for something.

"Well, actually," Shae said, "that's not true. I'm really not so good."

"What's the matter?"

"I..."

"What is it?"

Shae swallowed hard. "I... I don't really know how to tell you. I mean, you're going to think I sound crazy."

"What? No, no, I won't." *Did she want to come out to her?* The thought made her nervous. She slid her suddenly damp palms into her pockets. She wished they were alone, somewhere outside of her grandmother's earshot. "You want to take a walk or something?"

"Oh, um. Maybe...after."

"After what?"

"I actually came to talk to Ruby."

"Ruby? Oh." Fern hoped her disappointment didn't show. "She's in her studio. I can get her for you if you'd like."

"No, that's okay. I know the way."

Was it her imagination or was Shae walking so fast that she was practically running? *Running to get away from her?* Was it the conversation in the car? Why did she have to say anything about the letters? Hell, Shae probably didn't even remember her broken promise.

There were so many times Fern intended to write. She'd get as far as the salutation, and then she'd just stare at the net chasing some butterflies up the margin of her peach stationery.

It wasn't that she didn't have a million things to tell Shae. She did. Her new school was way different from her old one—

the itchy uniform with the penny loafers, all the teachers referring to the students by last name. "Yes, Ms. Beaumont." And her classmates talking about summer camp in the Catskills and violin lesson instead of fishing and swimming like in Louisiana. In fact, those first few weeks, Fern felt a little like those butterflies—furiously flapping her wings, not to get away but to catch up to those other girls, the ones who knew how to line their lids for that smoky look in the magazines. She wanted to tell Shae all of those things. But instead she'd just stared at those butterflies.

Maybe letter writing was hard because most of the time she and Shae communicated without words. A roll of the eyes meant *I am slowly dying listening to this adult talk.* A quirk of the brow meant *Why not? Sounds fun. You in?* A pat on the shoulder meant *It'll be okay.* And lacing their fingers together meant... *What had that meant?* What Fern remembered most about holding hands with Shae was the warmth...the safety.

Or maybe it wasn't about that. Maybe, if she was honest with herself, she'd admit that she'd wanted to leave Louisiana behind—for good. She'd spent most of that first year in New York dodging insults about Dixie flags and Cajun country. "Y'all eat squirrel down there?" one of the boys had asked her at recess. She spent more time crying in bathroom stalls than she did sitting in classrooms. She soon realized that if she just joined in, the insults stung less. But joining in meant that she was making fun of the people she'd loved—like Shae. She got good at it too, a regular comedian in fact, which made writing letters to Shae impossible. Every time she set a pen to paper, she felt sick to her stomach.

Fern's thoughts were interrupted by a commotion in the studio and then a shout. Although she couldn't make out the words, it sounded something like she imagined an 1840s Sacramento miner would yell at the very moment he spotted a golden nugget in his sifter. And then the door swung open. Ruby emerged with Shae in tow. She was walking so quickly that Shae had to break into little jogs to keep up.

"You drive, dear. I'm too anxious," she said as she fumbled through what Fern had quickly learned was the junk drawer in the kitchen island where Ruby kept an assortment of things like golf tees, scissors, twisty ties, glue, tape, postage stamps, and keys. The drawer reminded Fern of a vintage cartoon character she'd seen on the Nickelodeon Channel when she was a kid: a caveman who looked like a ball of hair with feet, arms, eyes, and a nose. He could pull any number of things out of that hair—a magnifying glass, a frying pan, even a sofa. Like his hair, Ruby's drawer contained endless items. In addition to those already mentioned, Fern had seen that drawer produce spatulas, screwdrivers, and even a small box of neon yellow modeling clay.

"Where are you going?" Fern asked.

"To see Lilith."

"Who's Lilith?"

"I'll explain on the way," Ruby said, placing the keys in Shae's open palm and simultaneously hitting the drawer closed with her hip. "Go on now, get your shoes on," she said to Fern.

"I'm going with you?"

"*Yes*," she said as if exasperated. "Now hurry up!"

Fern did as instructed and followed the two women out to the car.

Ruby gave Shae turn-by-turn instructions through the town and in between answered Fern's questions.

"Her name is Lilith, and she's the… Oh, it's a right at the stop sign up ahead." She pointed. "Anyway, as I was saying, Lilith's a medicine woman of sorts."

Fern turned to Shae and without even hiding the concern in her voice, said, "You are sick then."

"No, I'm not. I've just been having these…visions."

"Visions?"

Ruby shielded the late afternoon sun from her eyes with her hand. "There at that sign. Turn there." The sign read "Find out if there really is life after death. Trespass on this property."

"Are you sure?" Shae asked.

"Yes, I'm sure," Ruby snapped. "It's just down there." She pointed down an ominous looking dirt road, one that, with its tall weeds and underbrush, would be the perfect place to hide a dead body.

"I think I saw this road on *Evil Lives Here*," Fern said, eliciting a nervous laugh from Shae.

When they emerged from the trees, she saw a wooden cabin on stilts. The part facing them was small enough to be mistaken as a shack, but as they got closer, more of the house came into view. It was much deeper than it seemed. A wooden dinghy hung from its side. Dwarfed by the length of the house, it looked like a lifeboat attached to the side of a cruise ship. And it probably was a lifeboat of sorts—ready to set sail if the river flooded. In keeping with the theme, an orange lifesaver ring decorated the cabin's door and a large square vintage sign filled the wall to its right. It read "Lil's Swamp Tours" in a bold seventies font that was probably once red and was now a faded and weathered pink. The title was superimposed on the picture of a cartoon alligator holding a fork in one hand and a knife in the other. Tied around the alligator's neck was a bib adorned with a couple stick-figure men. The caption that ran across the bottom said, "Please do not feed yourself to the gators. Keep arms and legs in the boat at all times."

Fern scanned the trees and brush. "Where's the water?"

"It's down aways—past the cemetery."

"Cemetery?" Shae parroted, a noticeable quake in her voice.

"Oh nothing too scary. Just a pet cemetery."

The girls laughed in unison.

"That's a Stephen King movie," Fern said.

"What is?"

"*Pet Sematary*."

Ruby shook her head. "If you girls didn't watch so many horror movies, you wouldn't be scared out of your wits every time you hear a cricket chirp."

Fern's gaze passed over the yard, if it could be called that. It was filled with weeds, dirt, and junk that had obviously been left in the elements for quite some time. A rusted metal rooster lay face down, half buried in the mud. An old deflated beach ball whose color had chipped off in places held small pools of dirty rainwater, and a horizontal orange traffic cone was smashed in as if backed over with a truck tire. "I doubt anyone's here, Grandma. It looks like the place was abandoned a long time ago."

Ruby ignored her, the wood of the porch creaking under the weight of each of her steps. She knocked. There was no answer.

Surprise, surprise, Fern thought.

Ruby reached for the knob.

"What are you—?" Before she could finish her sentence, she found herself staring through the now open door into the cabin's interior, which was shockingly different than its dilapidated outside. The wood floors were polished to an almost reflective shine. The kitchen was modern with a soapstone sink and a quartz countertop. An old cast iron teakettle with a coiled handle sat on the gas stovetop, still steaming from a recent brew. On the round table in the center of the room sat three delicate teacups on saucers—cups that reminded Fern of her Aunt Nelly's house with its doily decorations and butterscotch candy smell. *What the hell?*

"Lilith's work space is in the back room," Ruby said. Fern had expected the back room to be down the hallway, but Ruby made no move in that direction. Instead, she walked to the sink. On the wall over the sink was a line of spice-filled test tubes with cork stoppers. She removed the tube fourth from the left of the spice rack. Then, like magic, a hidden door in the wood paneled wall—previously camouflaged by the grain and the pattern—swung open.

Fern's jaw dropped.

"What the hell?" Shae said.

"Fenugreek," Ruby said.

"What?"

"It's mostly for controlling blood sugar. They used to use it to induce labor, too."

"Umm, the wall, Grandma—not the spice."

"Oh." She laughed. "Lilith is quite secretive."

"Ya think?" Fern studied the inside of the door, a half-full bookcase. She didn't recognize any of the titles: *Women Who*

*Run with Wolves, Wicca Craft, Spiral Dance, Solitary Witch...
Witch?* "Who is this woman?"

"Lilith!" Ruby yelled into the interior, her voice echoing
against the walls.

"I've been expecting you!" a disembodied voice said in
return. "There's tea on the counter. Help yourselves!"

Fern turned back to the three cups. *How did she know there
were three of us?* Shae's matching surprised expression suggested
she was wondering the same thing.

Ruby took the middle cup between her hands and breathed
in its scent. "Oolong, my favorite," she said, sighing contentedly.
Shae and Fern followed suit.

"How did this Lilith know we were coming?" Fern asked.
"Did you text her or something?"

"She doesn't need a text, dear." Ruby laughed. "It's her
business to know. She's a psychic."

Fern almost choked on her tea, already doctored with just
the right amount of milk and honey.

A sound from the hidden doorway drew her attention there.
The woman who emerged was wearing a turban headscarf
in a bohemian style. Her long silver hair extended out from
the scarf's bottom and fell onto her shoulders in soft natural
waves. She wore a colorful Guatemalan skirt that swished and
shimmered as she moved. And she was barefoot, her toes painted
a deep blue color, each nail decorated with little sparkly stars.

"I'm Lilith but my Wiccan name is Danu," she said, reaching
out her hand for a shake, her braceleted arms jingling like wind
chimes. "You must be Shae, the admirable." Taking in Shae's
perplexed expression, she added, "Your name, Shae. It's Gaelic.
It means admirable. And you," Lilith said, turning to Fern, "you
are Ruby's granddaughter, Fernanda, the adventurous."

"More like, Fern, the nonflowering plant."

"Fern," she said as if tasting its letters like wine notes, "the
lover of shade."

Fern shrugged.

She returned to Shae. "I understand you need a spirit guide."

"Yeah. I mean, I think. I've had visions of—"

"Alia Ambrois—the missing girl."

The girl on the news? Fern felt a chill despite it being a comfortable seventy degrees and rubbed her arms with her hands to warm them. She looked to Shae for answers, but Shae looked just as lost and confused as she felt.

Lilith clapped her hands together in one loud smack, causing all three heads to turn in her direction. The suddenness of the sound brought Fern fully awake, as if before it, she had slumbered through her life in a semiconscious state. Lilith was like one of those party magicians who hypnotizes unsuspecting audience members and then wakes them with the ding of a bell or the snap of fingers. Fern checked the time on her phone and was relieved that she hadn't lost minutes or hours, at least as far as she could tell.

"Well, then, let's get started, shall we?" Lilith gestured her guests into the hidden door from which she'd come.

The room had a surreal rosy glow. The decor was eclectic— all antiques but from different time periods and places. A Louis XV armchair complete with walnut frame and needlepoint upholstery, a mustard colored fainting couch, and two plush Victorian parlor chairs. With each step into the room, Fern felt like she'd jumped through time by the decade.

The competing patterns and colors had a dizzying effect. The wool area rug had ancient Egyptian motifs in ivory and rust, a bookcase made of milk crates was covered in a shiny purple runner, the fabric of which could be a dress for either a Gatsby party or an 80's prom. Two floor lamps—one with a pink fringed shade reminiscent of brothels in the old West, and the other with Tiffany glass in a Navajo Mission design— flanked the makeshift bookcase. If that wasn't bad enough, the room's solitary window was obscured by shimmering sequined curtains, with a string of white Christmas lights, blinking on and off intermittently like an army of fireflies, affixed to its frame.

Lilith motioned to the fainting couch. "You and Ruby can sit here."

Fern couldn't help but laugh as she took a seat.

"What's so funny?" Ruby asked.

"Your granddaughter might just know a little something about this piece's history," Lilith said, placing a hand on the couch's tufted upholstery.

Both Ruby and Shae looked confused.

"In the 1800s," Lilith explained, "the fainting couch was used as part of a home treatment for female hysteria, a condition blamed for all sorts of ailments and behaviors, many of which, I should add, were completely normal and healthy. Irritability, for example." She leaned toward Shae, and whispered, "And sexual frustration. There were a lot of crazy…" She made imaginary quotation marks in the air with her fingers. "…cures for hysteria. Like pelvic massages, and in very severe cases, vibrators." She winked. "Hence, the need for comfortable sofas for long treatment sessions."

"And why do you have one?" Fern asked.

"This pseudoscience may seem like ancient history, but hysteria wasn't actually removed from the *DSM* until the early eighties."

"*DSM?*"

"*The Diagnostic and Statistical Manual of Mental Disorders*— the bible of psychiatry. I keep this couch, Fern, to remind me of how science is not…an exact science." She laughed. "Enough nostalgia," she said, directing her attention at Shae. "It seems you have an assignment."

"But how did you—"

"How did I know that's what Josephine called them?"

Shae nodded.

"You're not the only one who came in search of a spirit guide."

"Grandma's been here?"

"Oh, yes. Many times. Only here wasn't exactly here and I wasn't exactly me."

"What?"

"Let's save that story for another day. Today is about you."

CHAPTER SIX

"Purple purpurite." Lilith placed a large stone on the table in front of Shae. "It allows us to hear them better."

"Them?" Shae folded her hands in her lap to keep her fingers from trembling. She'd felt a sense of dread ever since they'd arrived, as if a Mack truck was barreling toward them, and would, at any moment, squash them and the little house like a garlic press.

"The spirits."

"What spirits exactly?" Shae asked. "Alia isn't..." She swallowed the word *dead* before it left her lips. For all she knew, the girl could be dead by now.

Lilith walked to the bookshelf. "Spirits can sometimes see things that we can't," she said as she crouched down to dig through a cardboard box. "Your spirit guide may be able to help you on your quest to find Alia."

"How does this work exactly? I mean, how do we find this guide?"

"Ah, here they are," she said, ignoring Shae's question. She stood, something cradled in her hands. "The correct question is how will *you* find the guide. I won't be going with you."

"Okay then, how will I find him?"

"You'll journey to the Alter Plane," she said, emptying her hands on the table in front of them.

Shae stared at the other colored stones that joined the purple purpawhatever. "Alter what?"

"It's a place between here and there."

What is she, the Riddler? "I get that it's a place where the spirits are, but where is it?"

"Actually, most spirits aren't there. Most cross over."

"And some don't have bus fare?" Fern joked.

Lilith shot Fern a look. "The spirits who dwell in the Alter Plane, Shae, have not yet been able to break with the material world—to accept the transition."

"Why not?"

"It could be any number of things. But most are simply not at peace. Something for them remains unresolved."

"But what does that have to do with me finding my spirit guide? Are you saying the guide is one of these disgruntled ghosts?"

Lilith frowned. "The spirits that dwell in the Alter Plane must earn their way across. If your spirit guide is successful in helping you, then she may be granted access to the other realm."

"So much for selfless spirits." Fern laughed.

"You'll need tools for your journey," Lilith said, ignoring the interruption. "Please, give me your hands."

Shae did as instructed and Lilith placed a black stone in her right palm.

"Smokey quartz." Shae slid her thumb over its smooth glasslike surface. "It's a grounding stone," Lilith explained.

"Grounding?"

"We're going to be doing some work that requires you to be…untethered, so to speak. This stone will help you find your way back to us."

"Will this work when I'm…um…skinwalking? Will it help me get back?"

Lilith shook her head. "We don't know why Skinwalkers come and go as they do." Lilith pointed to the stone in Shae's palm. "But if you float away in the Alter Plane, this will help you find your way back."

Shae felt nervousness flare inside her as she thought of a balloon disappearing into the sky. "I'm not sure about this."

"When you feel like you're too far from us—from you—close your fingers around this stone. Take your shoes off and dig your toes into the earth."

"What?" *Take my shoes off? Just how crazy is this woman?*

Lilith lifted the tablecloth to reveal her own bare feet, her nails like tiny solar systems. "Making contact with the earth through your feet is a good way to ground yourself," she said. "It helps if you imagine that you're a tree and that your roots stretch from the soles of your feet deep into the earth. The warmth of Mother Gaia will wind its way—"

"Okay, just hold on!" Shae let go of the stone. It bounced once and tumbled onto the fanned deck of tarot cards. The card on which the stone came to rest pictured a man with golden hair set ablaze, little wavy lines forming a yellow lion's mane around his head. One of his legs was bent at the knee and crossed behind the other. Both of his arms were akimbo. The words that ran across the top of the card were upside down: The Hanged Man. Wonderful, Shae thought.

She turned to Ruby and Fern. Her outburst had apparently ended their conversation and now their eyes and attention were fixed on Shae and the table. "Are you guys buying this stuff?" she asked.

Fern shrugged. Ruby squinted at her as if she were trying to read the print on a prescription bottle. "Of course I am," she said. The certainty in Ruby's voice was as solid as if Shae had asked if she believed in the air, the moon or life itself. "This *stuff* can save Alia's life."

Alia's life. If Alia Ambrois was really in that shack, didn't Shae owe it to her to try her best to find her, even if that meant squeezing rocks and imagining tree roots growing out of her feet? Shae turned back to Lilith then, who looked more tired than before. "I'm sorry," she said as she took up the stone in her fingers.

"It's a lot to digest. I know." Lilith pointed to the card with the man whose hair was on fire. "The Hanged Man…in reverse." She looked at Shae, her eyes filled with compassion. "There is a message that you have not heeded. And when we don't learn something we are supposed to, Shae, it returns to us until we do. Each time it becomes more challenging than the last."

"What lesson?"

"Only you know that." Lilith held another stone out to Shae, this one a translucent green. "Calcite," she said. "For protection."

"What do I need protection from?"

"Not all the spirits are good. Some may try to get you to stay in that plane. You mustn't believe the spirits you encounter there."

"I don't understand. I thought one of them was my spirit guide?"

"Who says your spirit guide is a person?"

"What?"

Lilith ignored the question. She turned her palms face up in front of her and fixed her eyes on Shae. It took Shae a moment to realize the meaning of the gesture—that she was waiting for her to take her hands. Shae slid the stones into the front pocket of her jeans and placed her palms on top of Lilith's. Lilith shut her eyes and gently closed her fingers around Shae's hands. She began chanting incoherent words. The chant sounded sorrowful, like the cry of a mother whale separated from her young. Whatever the woman was trying to do wasn't working. Nothing was happening except Shae was growing more embarrassed by the second.

But there wasn't long for her to feel foolish. Soon she spiraled through a dark funnel cloud toward a mere dot of light below her. The dot's circumference grew exponentially larger as she tumbled toward it. Then it enveloped her. She squeezed her eyes shut and braced herself for whatever was coming, which turned out to be the ground. Shoulder first, she slammed into asphalt and rolled a few feet before coming to a stop. Pain pulsed angrily in the right side of her body, from her hip to her neck. Before she had the chance to inventory her injuries, the blast of a car horn practically stopped her heart.

"What the hell are you doing?" an angry male voice yelled.

Shae blinked into the car's blinding headlights.

"Well, don't just sit there! Get the hell out of the road!"

Shae sat up and felt a wrenching pain in her right shoulder. She was in the middle of a street but not any street that she recognized. It was nighttime—and snowing. In the arc of the car's headlamps, she could see the street was dusted white and she felt the cold sting of flakes landing on her cheeks and nose. Her gaze was immediately drawn to a street lamp about a kilometer behind the car. It looked ancient with its decorative post and incandescent globes. *What is this place?* "Sorry," she muttered, trying to shield the car's bright lights from her eyes with the side of her hand. "I don't know how I got here. I was just…" *Sitting at some hippie lady's table listening to a whale cry.* "I'm sorry," she said again and pushed herself erect.

"Well, get the hell out of my way, Skinwalker!" he barked.

"What?"

The driver grumbled something incoherent but unmistakably angry and then she heard the hum of the window being closed.

She made her way to the side of the road but not quickly enough for him. Before she'd even stepped foot on the shoulder, she felt a rush of air as the car barreled past her, the horn blaring again as it passed. She searched the horizon for a house, a store, anywhere she could get help. And then she saw it. Just outside the reach of the streetlights was a pair of glowing orbs—perfectly round and bright greenish yellow—hovering about twenty-five inches off the ground.

"Hello?" she asked tentatively, her half-frozen fingers trying unsuccessfully to work the zipper of her sweatshirt.

The orbs swung from side to side but remained perfectly aligned as if they were the ends of a tiny barbell. Was this one of the nonhuman spirits that Lilith was talking about? She felt in her pocket for the stone—the protective one. Her fingers easily recognized it by its rough and jagged feel. Despite its protection, the orbs moved closer or grew in size, she wasn't sure which. She took a step back. And then she was sure. They were definitely moving closer. Adrenaline coursed through her body, making her pulse quicken and the hair on her arms stand on end. She turned and took off running. A sharp sound like a dog's bark slowed her movement. And then there was another one. It was definitely a bark. It was just a dog, its eyes reflecting the moonlight.

"It's okay," she said, bending down on one knee and extending her arms in what she hoped was a nonthreatening stance. "Come here, doggie. It's okay." She could tell from the way the orbs disappeared and reappeared that the dog was pacing back and forth—sizing her up, perhaps.

"Come on, sweetie. It's okay," she said again. "I won't hurt you. I promise." The promise must've been enough because the large ball of fur bounded into her arms and licked her cheeks, chin, and nose. She recognized the breed—Siberian husky. He was mostly white with a blend of black and gray on his head and down his back. He had one light blue eye. The other was brown. "Aren't you handsome?" she cooed and ran her fingers through his thick mane. He wasn't wearing a tag or collar, but he was friendly enough as she had to literally push him away to avoid a saliva bath.

"What are you doing out here all alone?" she asked. He wagged his tail in response. And then he jumped from her arms and did a little a circular dance before stopping to face her again. He cocked his head to the side as if listening.

"What is it, boy?"

A bark. Then another. And then he did a curious thing. He turned away from her, trotted a few paces, and turned back, tilting his head as he had before. He stood stock-still and glared at her as if waiting for the stupid human to get the message.

"What do you want?"

He repeated the same motions— walking a few feet in the opposite direction and then turning back again.

She stood. He barked excitedly as if to say, "Yes, that's it," and then trotted ahead, stopping periodically to check behind him to see if she was still following.

She followed him through a field and down several neighborhood streets. He stopped at a wrought-iron gate. An arc of lettering across its top read *Caulfield Cemetery*. She could see obelisk tombstones in the distance. If the snow wasn't proof enough, she could now be absolutely certain that she wasn't in Louisiana. In most Louisiana cemeteries, the dead are buried in aboveground tombs; otherwise, the caskets would be floating.

The dog barked again and nosed the gate.

She glanced back at the obelisks, seeming to grow out of the ground like odd, creepy vegetables. The scene was horror-movie eerie—a graveyard at night, the cold whispering wind, and everything covered in a blanket of white. "I don't really want to go in there," she said. "What do you say we just take a walk?"

The dog clasped one of the bars in his teeth. "Can't we talk about this?" Digging his back paws into the dirt for leverage, he yanked at the gate. It didn't budge. Shae could see that it was closed with a fork latch.

"Well, don't hurt yourself," she said, lifting the latch with one finger. "The human hand." She wiggled her fingers. "Very helpful." The dog audibly sighed. She laughed and swung the gate open.

The dog wasted no time and ran past her, his tail and ears standing straight up, as if on high alert.

"Hey, wait up!" Seeming not to hear her, the dog continued barreling forward. Shae had to jog to keep up.

She was almost out of breath when he finally came to a stop in front of a marble gravestone. She used her palm to wipe enough of the snow away to read the marker, barely visible in the light of a distant street lamp: *Beloved daughter and sister Katherine Anne Biggs July 10, 2007 – March 16, 2019. Precious*

Child. Our hearts still ache in sadness and secret tears still flow. What it meant to lose you, no one will ever know. "She was just a kid." The dog rubbed its muzzle against the grave marker.

"But why are you showing me this?"

The dog turned his head to the side and studied her.

"I don't understand."

He pawed the gravestone, his nails making a scratchy sound against the marble.

"What is it?"

"He can't talk," a male voice said, making her heart leap into a panic.

"Who's there?" she managed, turning toward the sound.

A man dressed in a double-breasted striped jacket and straw boater hat stood leaning against a nearby tree. She wondered how long he'd been there.

"Tonal imitations," he said.

She stared blankly.

"I mean they can imitate tones, make vowel sounds mostly, but they can't use their tongues and lips for consonants. Try saying *puppy* without your lips. You'll see what I mean." When the man smiled, his ultra-thin Rudolph Valentino mustache formed a straight line across his upper lip. He tipped his hat, revealing a head of well oiled, slicked back hair and did a little bow. "The name's Milton Wetherby."

"Hello, Mr. Wetherby. I'm Shae. Shae Williams."

"Miss Williams," he said, taking her hand in his. "A pleasure." His mustache tickled the back of her hand as he pressed it to his lips. "You must forgive me as I've had a jorum of skee tonight at the juice joint and am half-seas over."

"You what?"

"Don't tell me you're a dry crusader?"

She blinked. "A dry what?"

"Ab-so-lute-ly!" He laughed, his round belly jiggling with the movement.

"Mr. Wetherby, do you happen to know a family around here named Ambrois?"

"Ambrois?" He rubbed his chin between his fingers. "I can't rightly say I do. Are you a relative of theirs?"

"Not a relative, no. I'm looking for a missing girl. Her name is…" The name, which had just been on the tip of her tongue, inexplicably vanished. "I don't… I don't remember. What was I saying?"

Mr. Wetherby flashed her a brilliant smile. "You were about to ask me if there was speakeasy nearby."

"I was?" She didn't remember that. In fact, she thought there was something much more important she was supposed to do here.

"And as a matter fact," he said, "there is one—just around the corner." He smiled again. "Shall we go then?"

The urgency of before was all but forgotten now. "I'd love to!" The words were formed by her lips and tongue, the air expelled from her lungs, but she didn't…think them. And yet there they were nonetheless.

"Fabulous!" he said, hooking her arm in the crux of his.

As they neared the gate through which she had entered the cemetery, he said, "I seem to have left my wallet. Would you be a good chap and buy us a dram?"

Shae reached into her pocket, her fingers closing around something round and smooth. A stone. What was a stone doing in here? And then it all came rushing back…the dog, the grave marker, Alia, Lilith. *You mustn't believe the spirits you encounter there.* Shae pulled her arm free. "I'm afraid I can't stay."

Mr. Wetherby's smile melted as if it were made of wax and Shae's words burning embers.

"You Skinwalkers," he spat. "You're all the same!"

"You've met people like me before?"

His answer came in a burst of deep hearty laughter. "What is this? Your first life?"

She stared blankly. *First life?*

"Leave her alone, Wetherby!"

Shae turned around. There within arm's distance, stood a woman, a beautiful woman, with plump dark lips and raven black hair. She was dressed in skintight leather pants that showed off her curves, a white ruffle blouse, and a fitted motorcycle jacket. "Don't you have anything better to do than play with the cemetery visitors?"

Without saying anything, he tipped his hat courteously and backed away, disappearing into the darkness.

"Thanks," Shae said.

"Don't mention it." The woman eyed her suspiciously. "You don't look like the average Skinwalker."

"No? What does one look like?"

"You're just so…" The woman's hazel eyes rolled up Shae's body, leaving the skin that they touched electrified.

"Young?"

"I was going to say attractive but young works too," she said and smiled. "I'm Yasmine."

"Shae."

"So, Shae." She made her name sound like a purr. "Why don't you tell me why you're lurking around our little spirit playground?"

"I jumped or Skinwalked or whatever you call it into a girl named Alia Ambrois. She's been kidnapped."

Yasmine's forehead crinkled in concern. "And she was murdered?"

"No." Shae considered. "Well, I mean, I don't know."

"But you think she's here?"

"I hope not."

Yasmine looked confused.

"I came here to find my spirit guide. I was told that he could help."

"And did you find him?"

She looked around for the dog, who seemed to have disappeared with Mr. Wetherby's arrival. "I think so."

"And did he tell you what you needed to know?"

"He doesn't talk—intonation issue."

Yasmine smiled. "Yes, spirit guides take on the shape of animals."

"What animal are you?"

Yasmine quirked an eyebrow. "Sadly, I'm still bipedal. Let's just say I'm getting used to the place, still learning the ropes."

"Oh, yeah? How long have you been here?"

"Since nineteen sixty-four."

Shae gasped.

"Why, what year are you coming from?"

"Two thousand nineteen."

Yasmine sighed. "Slow learner." She shook her head as if to free herself of the thought. "So, what did your spirit animal show you then? I love a good mystery."

"He showed me a grave of someone else...Katherine Anne Biggs. She died this year. I mean my...this year."

"So, you think your kidnapper is this Katherine's killer?"

"I don't know. Maybe," she said, considering.

"Well, I suggest if you got what you need that you don't hang out too much longer. There are some pretty unsavory characters here."

"Oh yeah? Are you...an unsavory character?"

"I was. I mean, I can be." She ground some snow with the heel of her boot. "But right now..." She raised her eyes to look at Shae. "I guess I don't want to be."

"I'm glad."

Yasmine smiled. "Maybe I'll do some digging and see what I can find out about your Katherine Biggs."

"Do you think she could be here?"

"No. Most kids are innocents. They cross over."

"Why haven't you...um...crossed over?"

"Hell if I know." She shrugged.

"I'll come back then...to see what you found out."

Yasmine smiled. "Who knows, I might be a Pomeranian by then." She laughed.

Shae joined her. "I don't know how to leave," she said awkwardly.

"You squeeze that grounding stone in your pocket."

"You can see what's in my pocket?"

"I'm a spirit, Shae."

She squeezed the stone.

"It helps if you take your shoes off," Yasmine said.

"Are you serious?"

"No, silly," she said. "I overheard your conversation. The Medicine Woman has a portal to this plane, so I sometimes catch bits and pieces of her conversation."

Shae wrapped her fingers around the stone. "I'm squeezing it, now what?"

"Imagine something you want to get back to—in your world. Is there something? Or someone?"

"Fern." The first thing that came to her mind was Fern's sandy hair and creamy skin. And those chameleon eyes of hers that, with her mood, could leap through the blue spectrum from gunmetal to china faster than a snow cone melts in the summer sun. She smiled despite herself.

Shae blinked her eyes open and Yasmine and the cemetery and the snow were gone. She was back in her chair at the table in Lilith's hidden room, the grounding stone still pressed in her palm.

"That woman may not be trustworthy," Lilith said.

"Who? What?"

Lilith frowned. "Be careful. She's not a spirit guide yet, probably for good reason. Don't mistake attraction for trust."

Shae's gaze found Fern's in that moment, eyes turned dark—the color of denim. It was a shade Shae had never seen before and wondered what it meant.

She? She who? Fern had imagined the spirits to be glowing opaque shapes glimmering in and out of space and time like light. She hadn't considered that the shapes could be attractive, let alone female. The thought of Shae ogling some ghost woman made her teeth clench and her fingers close into tight fists.

"You could hear us?" Shae asked Lilith. "In the other plane?"

"Our hands were joined. Our energies intertwined."

Shae glanced in Fern's direction. The nervousness in her expression, the apology in her eyes made Fern wonder, yet again, if Shae could read her mind—if she could see... What was it? Anger? Jealousy? And why would she be jealous? So what if Shae has the hots for some ghost woman? Or real woman for that matter. That didn't affect her at all.

"So, yes," Lilith continued, "I could *sense* what you were feeling, but *we* couldn't hear what you were saying."

A look of relief flashed in Shae's eyes.

"So, what did you learn about Alia?" Ruby asked.

"I didn't."

Probably too busy with the spirit girl, Fern thought snidely.

"I mean," Shae corrected, "I didn't learn anything about Alia specifically, but the spirit guide showed me something that might be related."

"Something?" Lilith parroted.

"Well, someone. A gravestone of a girl named Katherine Anne Biggs. She died just six months ago. And she's buried in the Caulfield Cemetery."

"I've never heard of Caulfield," Ruby said.

"We should do a search."

"Yeah, good luck with that," Fern said, remembering the single bar that vanished the moment they took the exit to the parish. She'd actually left her iPhone back on her nightstand and hadn't even bothered to plug it in. Here, it was little more than a really expensive address book.

"Who doesn't have Wi-Fi these days?" Lilith said with a laugh.

Fern eyed her grandmother and Ruby looked away uncomfortably.

Lilith showed the girls to her study, which was decked out with impressive techno-gadgets. She had everything from a Surface Pro 4 tablet to an iMac with not one, but two monitors positioned side by side.

Shae eyed the Magic Mouse warily.

"Not a Mac person?" Fern asked.

"Let's just say I'm no Mr. Robot."

She laughed and started typing. The Caulfield Cemetery was in Barnstable, Massachusetts, a touristy Cape Cod town.

"I don't understand. What does a girl's death in Massachusetts have anything to do with our missing Alia? I mean that's over a thousand miles from here," Shae said.

Fern did a search of the girl's name: *Katherine Anne Biggs*. A page of hits appeared on the screen. Her eyes caught on the phrases *Missing Mississippi Girl* and *Body Dragged from River*. "It looks like she's from Mississippi."

"I thought you said Massachusetts?"

"I did. I mean the cemetery's in Massachusetts." She pointed to the screen. "A Katherine Biggs died in Mississippi."

Reading from the article in the *Clarion-Ledger*, Fern said, "A nine-year-old Picayune girl was found dead in the lower Mississippi river eight days after being reported missing from a school science fair."

"Drowned?"

"Her death was described as 'suspicious.'"

"When did she die?"

Fern scanned the article, her finger sliding down the screen with her eyes until it stopped by a date.

"March sixteenth," Shae read. "The date on the grave. But why is she buried in Massachusetts?"

"Maybe there was a family burial plot at Caulfield or something," Fern offered, remembering the fight that broke out after her uncle's death. His third and first wives battled for two weeks over his final resting place. Wife number three wanted him in Pensacola near their home and wife number one wanted him in New Orleans where she lived with their daughter. Number one won. And Fern was happy that she did since it meant fewer trips to Florida for her.

She opened another window to search the distance between Picayune, where Katherine Biggs was found, and Algiers Point, where Alia Ambrois was taken. "Katherine died twenty-five minutes from here."

"Which means her killer could be the same guy who kidnapped Alia."

Fern did a search for convictions in the Katherine Anne Biggs murder case but found that there weren't any arrests. A mechanic and the son of some wealthy family had been brought in for questioning as persons of interest, but neither were charged. "They haven't found her killer. They never even ruled it a homicide." Fern felt a shiver run up her spine. "We should go to the police, Shae."

"And tell them what? That based on dream visions and a spirit dog, we've deduced that the same person killed Katherine and Alia?"

Fern frowned. "That doesn't sound so convincing, does it? Did you just say *dog*?"

Shae laughed. "Yeah, but that wasn't the spirit Lilith was talking about."

"Good. I thought you might be into bitches."

"Funny," Shae said drolly, looking more embarrassed than amused. After a beat, she added, "Desi told me...that you know. About me."

Fern nodded. "I..." She swallowed to give herself time to think. *What do people say?* She mined Shae's expression for answers but found none. "I don't even think about it. Honestly," she lied.

Shae smiled, relief settling her expression.

"It doesn't matter," Fern continued. "I mean, you're always just Shae to me." She smiled uneasily, worried that Shae would see right through her—right through to the truth that she'd not only been thinking about Shae being gay, she'd been obsessing about it, imagining Shae kissing girls, holding hands with girls, dancing with girls. Fern hid her now burning cheeks by turning away and looking again at the *Ledger* articles that filled the five open windows staring back at them.

"I'm really glad you feel that way. To be honest, I was worried about your reaction, with how close we were when we were kids, holding hands and—"

"I'm not gay." It was a reflex, unthinking and automatic. And, seeing how it made the light in Shae's eyes dim and turn inward, she wished she could take it back.

"I know," Shae said. "I wasn't implying... Look, I know we're just friends."

She couldn't stop the sadness from welling up within her, and she couldn't bring herself to look at Shae for fear that she would recognize her sadness too. Instead she kept her eyes glued to the screen. In her periphery she saw Shae stand and move away from her. The temperature seemed to drop as the distance between them grew.

"There's got to be something useful in those articles," Shae said from behind her.

She scanned the articles' titles and bylines and tried to focus on the words rather than how badly she'd bungled things with Shae. And then she saw it: Madeline Burch. The author's name appeared on three of the four articles. She clicked on the hyperlinked name and it took her to a list of recent and archived news articles by the author, as well as an option to *Send an E-mail to Madeline Burch*. "We could contact this reporter. She would obviously know a lot about the case."

"Brilliant!" Shae said, taking the seat next to her again.

She liked the praise almost as much as she liked the feel of Shae's elbow against her own. "Hey, I'm sorry I reacted like that before," she said.

"Don't worry about it." Shae shrugged. "It's pretty normal."

"What is?"

"You know, feeling like you have to make it clear that you're not like that so I don't hit on you."

"I wasn't worried that you'd…" A flash of heat stopped her words.

"Just because I'm gay, Fern, doesn't mean I'm into every woman I meet."

She blinked. "I didn't think you were into me."

Shae said nothing. Instead, she pinned her bottom lip between her teeth, pulling Fern's eyes with the movement. After a beat, she cleared her throat and said, "So, let's get that email out then."

Fern sensed that what was unsaid between them was much more important than that.

CHAPTER SEVEN

Ms. Burch's return email arrived two days later. After a few subsequent exchanges, they agreed to meet at a cafe on Verret Street in Algiers Point. It was one of those places where the food was from a macrobiotic farm and prepared by teenagers with ear gauges. A trendy place, its front door was painted with a local artist's rendition of "Starry Night." Outside seating included Pollockesque tablecloths, sculpture centerpieces made from kitchen utensils and sardine cans, and tattooed and pierced patrons looking stylishly maudlin and contemplative as they blinked into the artificial blue light of their cell phones.

It was exactly the kind of place that Desi would call "a one-hit wonder," after which he would hum a bar of "My Sharona" for effect. Looking around the cafe now, Shae guessed he was right. The place would probably last until the next big craze took hold and then fold like a house of cards as its fickle patrons developed a sudden and fashionable gluten-intolerance or a preference for coffee beans shat by civets.

Based on the photo on the *Ledger* website, Shae guessed that Madeline Burch was in her mid-to-late thirties. She had straight, strawberry blond hair—all one length—that hung limply to her shoulders like heavy drapes. Her longish bangs were brushed to the side, revealing a high forehead and an unusually pale but freckled complexion. Studious square frames sat high on the bridge of her nose, the thickness of their lenses distorting the shape of her head at the temples and lending her a slightly sunken look like an eggplant. In the photo Burch wore a black blazer with 1980s shoulder pads over a pink button-down shirt, the crisp collar lifting over the jacket lapels and jutting out into the sea of black like shark fins. The corners of her thin crimson lips were slightly curled, as if at the precise moment the camera's aperture closed, she was inwardly laughing at a private joke, probably at the photographer's expense.

Shae spotted the same straight, lifeless strawberry blond hair first. The woman sat with her back to them at a table in the far corner. A cow-print purse, which clashed with the paisley top she wore, hung from her chair back. It swung back and forth like a pendulum, jostled by a waiter attempting to navigate through the forest of tables and patrons. The movement caused the woman to turn toward the window, giving Shae a perfectly unobstructed view of her profile—upturned nose, smallish chin, and air of pompousness present in the slightly puckered bottom lip. It was definitely her. Madeline Burch was as unstylish as the café was trendy.

They made their way through the crowd. Close-up, she looked more wary than snooty. Her green eyes darted back and forth as if she were watching a Wimbledon volley, and her notably sensible shoe tapped an almost maniacal rhythm on the table leg.

"Ms. Burch?"

Her emerald eyes snapped to attention and landed first on Fern and then Shae.

"Please sit," she said through tight, unsmiling lips.

Shae took the seat opposite Ms. Burch and Fern took the one adjacent to her.

"Thank you for agreeing to meet with us, Ms. Burch," Fern said.

"What's this information you have for me?" She was clearly not much for small talk.

"You might have heard of a missing Algiers Point girl, Alia Ambrois?" Shae said.

"The runaway?"

"Alia didn't run away. She was taken."

The woman kinked an eyebrow. "By whom?"

"We think by the same man who killed Katherine Biggs."

"And you think this why?"

Fern glanced at Shae, sending her one of those, *I told you so* looks. And she had, in fact, told her so, *several* times on the car ride over.

"She's a reporter," Fern had said. "Of course she's going to press you for details."

"Yeah, and those details will have her walking in the opposite direction for sure."

"You'll just have to lie."

Shae shook her head. "I've never been a good liar."

Fern had reached across the center console and squeezed her thigh reassuringly. "I know. I remember," she said. She'd stared at Fern's hand—those long slender fingers cradling her thigh and heating her skin—and she silently wished that hand to explore further. But before she could fully entertain the notion, Fern jerked it away as if from a hot pan. The action was so abrupt and unsettling, that Shae wondered if her expression had betrayed her imaginings.

She now turned to Ms. Burch, her thigh still tingling with the memory of Fern's grasp. "It's complicated," she said, speaking of more than just Alia. "But please trust that we have reason to believe there's a connection."

Her lips flattened into an almost straight line, any hint of a smile that had been playing on her lips—whether snooty or nervous—vanished now and the wrinkles around her eyes and mouth deepened with what Shae suspected was annoyance or anger. It seemed as though she was going to leave. But she didn't. Instead, she said, "I thought you had something on the Copelands," sounding more disappointed than angry.

The name made the hair on Shae's arms stand up. *The boy at the bar. The boy with the Saints ball cap in his pocket.*

"Is that the wealthy family mentioned in your article?" Fern asked.

Madeline nodded.

"I thought their son had been cleared?"

"If by cleared you mean magically released after several titanic contributions to the police department, then yes, Boone was cleared."

"Are you saying his family bought his way out?"

Ms. Burch snorted. It was a loud, piercing sound to which any dogs in a five-mile radius would probably howl in response. "The Copelands' wealth and influence dates back to the nineteenth century. Their anchors are so deeply rooted in this town that their ship can't be budged, not by scandal and not by murder."

"So you think this Boone character murdered Katherine?" Shae asked.

"I *know* he murdered her," she said in a steady and convincing voice. "Witnesses placed him on or near the Biggs' property on several occasions. And this is Wallace, Louisiana, we're talking about. Ninety-four percent African American with a median household income of nineteen thousand. Boone, or any Copeland for that matter, had no business being there." Shae glanced at Fern, who looked completely riveted. "And his alibi…" She swiped angry quotation marks in the air. "…that he was home with his mother at the time of the murder? Please!"

"You don't think he was?" Fern asked.

"I think she could've easily lied for him. That family has a history of cover-ups."

"What do you mean?"

"This wasn't Boone's first rodeo," she said. "I wrote a story that exposed some of his less than favorable dealings with the police. All of which, I should add, had been magically expunged from his record. Not even a whole day after the story went live,

I was called into the editor-in-chief's office and pulled off the assignment. When I asked why, I was told that I was needed in fashion." She looked at them over her boxy plastic frames. "Do I look like someone who might be *needed* in fashion?"

Shae's glance took in the woman's flat Aerosol loafers. She laughed on cue. Madeline Burch was really starting to grow on her. "What sort of dealings with the cops?"

Ms. Burch leaned closer as if the patrons at the neighboring tables were listening. "Rape," she whispered, the same way that Shae's mother mouthed words like cancer and menopause, as if the softness with which they were uttered would somehow ensure their distance from the family. "A friend of his sister's."

"And he wasn't arrested?" Fern asked.

"I'm guessing you haven't seen the district attorney's office building in East Baton Rouge?"

Both Shae and Fern shook their heads.

"Beautifully renovated—another example of the Copelands' benevolence."

"So, these Copelands made contributions to avoid culpability?" Fern asked.

"Ooh, I like that alliteration," she said and clapped her hands excitedly, the first hint of a genuine smile playing on her face. "It would make a terrific headline." After a beat she added, "Too bad I'm too busy reporting on the more important stories involving bubble fingernails and pixelated hair." She snorted again, making Shae wince. "Listen," she said, regaining her composure. "I don't doubt that Boone could be involved in the Ambrois girl's kidnapping. But if he is, she may be gone already." She ran the pad of her index finger over a nick in the tabletop. "Katie was dead eight days after being taken. Thrown in the river like garbage."

Fern gasped audibly.

"Alia's alive," Shae said, without thinking.

Burch squinted in confusion, making Shae wish she could reel the words back in.

"She means we *hope* she's alive," Fern corrected.

Burch studied Shae for a moment longer. "Of course," she said. "We all hope that." She reached into the cow-print purse and produced a business card. "Some added luck," she said holding it in Shae's direction.

"What's this?"

"Just the name of a cop I used to know."

Under the Louisiana state banner was the name *Officer Elle Walker. Patrol Unit.*

"She might be able to help," Burch explained. "Elle's... well...resourceful." There was something about the way Burch said the officer's name that made Shae wonder if they had some sort of history together—of the romantic variety.

* * *

The Copeland house was a newly-renovated Victorian home located in the heart of New Orleans. Its high-peaked gables, angled bays, and square lattice windows made it a perfect addition to the Garden District, the elite neighborhood sandwiched between Central City and the Irish Channel. The area was originally developed in the mid-nineteenth century for those made wealthy on cotton and sugar, so it was no surprise that it now housed some of the best-preserved mansions in the Southeast, many of which had graced the covers of *Architectural Digest*. Multiple websites valued the Copeland's house at $2.2 million, noting several of its standout features—the original medallions, millwork and a heated saltwater pool.

The pool couldn't be seen from the street, though, where Shae and Fern sat observing the property from behind the windows of Ruby's Prius. And it was hard to imagine the place spanned the advertised eight thousand square feet.

Fern used her hand to clear away some of the fog from the passenger window. The Copeland's landscaping was lush with beds of jasmine and ivy, well placed and colorful star magnolias and Japanese maples, and a stately pergola with climbing roses. It looked as if it were lifted right from the pages of a storybook romance, and being in its presence, made her feel wistful. She couldn't help but smile.

"It's beautiful," she said.

"I guess." Shae shrugged. "If you like that sort of thing."

"What? Million-dollar homes?"

"The swag. That door knocker probably costs more than this car."

Fern hadn't noticed the knocker, although now that she saw it, she wondered how she could've missed it. It was a gold lion's head, the size of a pineapple. "Well, what kind of door knocker should they have on a two-million-dollar home?"

"Why do people with money insist on hanging it everywhere?" Shae asked as if she hadn't heard Fern's question.

"Are you saying that if you had that kind of money, you wouldn't spend it?"

Shae smirked. "I'm just saying I wouldn't be that indulgent on decorations."

"It sounds like you might have a thing against rich people. Maybe you don't like them *because* they're rich."

Shae faced her then, anger flashing in her eyes. "I what?"

"You're judging this family because of a silly trinket on their door."

"That silly trinket could probably feed a family of four for a year!"

"So? It's their money. And the Copelands can spend it however they want."

"*Their* money? Let's be real, Fern. This is old Louisiana money. That lion's head and whatever else looks glamorous about this place was bought on slave labor." Shae studied the door knocker again, her expression dour. "Capital gains," she mumbled. "The rich just keep getting richer."

Fern crossed her arms and turned away. While she understood Shae's feelings, she couldn't help but wonder if the slavery argument was convenient rather than valid. Sure, racism still existed, but things were markedly different. For one, America already had one president who was black. And it wasn't true that the rich stayed rich and the poor stayed poor. There were lots of rags to riches stories. "I happen to think this is the land of opportunity. Look at Bill Gates. He never even graduated from college!"

"He dropped out of Harvard. *Harvard.*"

"But he came from humble beginnings."

"The son of a prominent lawyer?"

"Maybe it's Steve Jobs I'm thinking of."

"Who went to expensive Reed College?"

Feeling at a loss, she bit her lip. She couldn't think of an example. She was sure there was one, though.

"Look, I don't want to argue with you," Shae said, her eyes softening. "You and I, we come from different backgrounds. And because of that, we have different perspectives on this stuff."

She narrowed her eyes. "We grew up in the same neighborhood."

"But your parents had money. And that money sent you to college."

She blinked.

"I mean, look at your clothes."

"What about my clothes?" She hid her Dolce and Gabbana sunglasses from view.

"It doesn't matter. Look, we're just different."

She felt hot with anger. "Are you saying I'm privileged?"

Shae studied her for a moment and then blew out a breath. "All I'm saying is we're different." She turned back to the Copeland's house as if to end the conversation.

But Fern wasn't ready to let the matter rest. "Did it ever occur to you that the Copelands might give back? That they don't just sit on their money hoarding it?"

"They do give back," Shae said, surprising Fern. "They bought the district attorney a building."

She couldn't help but laugh, thankful for the release of tension. "So," she asked, happy to change the subject, "Do you recognize anything...from your dream?"

Shae squinted as she studied the house's perimeter, well-manicured shrubs and flowering trees on a vast plot of land.

"Nah," she said. "It wasn't here. The place I was…I mean, *Alia* was, was dilapidated. There was graffiti on the walls."

"Then it's probably not too far from civilization." Fern popped the glove compartment open. "Is there any paper in here?" she asked, rifling through its contents.

"For what?"

"A petition."

"A petition for what?"

"Not for what…for whom."

"Huh?"

"Let's meet him."

"Who? *Boone?*"

"Yes, Boone. Who do you think?" She found a sheet of paper and used the side of her hand to iron out the kinks. "I wish we had a clipboard or something."

"How about a folder?" Shae asked, reaching her hand behind the passenger seat.

"That'll work."

Fern used a pen she found in the glove box to fill half of the paper with phony names and phone numbers.

"I don't think this is a good—"

"Just trust me," she said and squeezed Shae's hand.

As they made their way up the Copeland's flagstone walkway, Fern tried to convey in the smile she directed at Shae the confidence she wished she was feeling, the confidence she should be feeling. But she couldn't hide the slight tremor in her fingers as she reached for the ring in the lion's mouth. Within seconds of the first hollow knock, the door was pulled open from the inside.

"Can I help you?" A round gray-haired woman stood in the doorway, wiping her hands on her frilly white apron.

"Hi there," Fern said, flashing the best sorority girl smile she could muster—a combination of brainless and blessed. "We'd like to speak with Boone if he's available."

The woman's skeptical gaze scanned Fern's companion from toe to brow, a slight downturned mouth suggesting either disbelief or disgust. "And what business do you have with Mr. Copeland?" she asked, her eyes disconcertedly fixed on Shae.

"I…" Shae muttered. *It was true. Lying was her kryptonite.*

Fern held the paper and folder out for the woman to inspect. "We have a petition. We'd like his support."

"What sort of petition?" she asked in a voice filled with suspicion as she scanned the list of fictitious names and numbers Fern had penned in the car.

"We're trying to keep Sigma Omega Delta from having to move off campus." Her gaze relaxed from a full-on squint to what looked like drowsiness. *It was working.* "After our last… um…get-together, the dean revoked our campus housing permit."

"You're from Tulane?" An almost smile.

Fern nodded. The woman's gaze floated over to Shae once again, who was, to Fern's dismay, standing numbly at her side with about as much animation as a coat rack. So very sorority girl, Fern thought drolly. The woman may have agreed, given that her expression transformed from polite but constipated to disdainful. Fern nudged Shae with her elbow. She must've gotten the hint because she kicked out one foot as if she were a Rockette and said, "Go Riptide!"

"Come in," the woman said, seemingly satisfied. "I'll see if he's available."

The girls stepped through the threshold and into the foyer. The expensive wood floor was so polished that, in the light of the crystal chandelier overhead, it reflected an almost mirror image of the antique grandfather clock in the corner. A luxurious, curved staircase with elaborately carved molding and handrails wound around the wall on which the clock was positioned. Large framed paintings lit by museum-style fixtures filled each wall. Throwing one or two furtive glances their way, the woman disappeared up the stairwell.

"How did you know that would work?" Shae whispered when they were alone.

Fern shrugged. "He's twenty and rich. He's got to be in college somewhere."

"Sigma Omega Delta? Is that even real?"

"It was in *Big Fish*."

Shae bit her lip, her eyebrows dipping in concern.

"It'll be fine."

The woman returned a few moments later with a medium-size dog at her heels. Fern recognized it as a German shorthaired pointer. As a versatile hunting dog in both the field and the water, the GSP was pretty popular in bayou country. She was a pretty one, too, with a sleek chocolate brown coat, a deep chest, and strong quarters.

"Hi pup," she cooed as the dog bounded toward her with its tongue wagging.

Shae seemed to have an entirely different reaction to the dog. All the blood seemed to drain from her face. She took a tentative step back as if she feared the dog would lunge with too fast of a movement.

"Oh don't be scared of Bella here," the woman said, eyeing Shae and scratching behind the dog's ears. She wagged her tail obediently in response. "She's a regular pussycat. Unless of course you're being hunted." She winked.

Shae looked like she might be sick.

"I'm afraid you girls just missed Boone. He left for target practice with the shooting club."

"Sh...shooting club?" Shae repeated, her voice cracking like a prepubescent boy.

"That's okay," Fern said, eyeing Shae warily. "We'll catch up with him later I'm sure."

As soon as they closed the car door, Shae was talking, words firing out of her like a semiautomatic machine gun. "That was the dog! The same dog! The dog from my dream!"

"Slow down. What are you talking about?"

"Boone...the target practice! The hat! He's the guy, Fern! Alia was being chased through the woods. Hunted. She was being hunted! And Boone is the guy!"

Fern was scared. "We've got to go to the police." This was too much for the two of them to handle alone. "Do you still have that card the reporter gave you with the officer's name?"

Fern saw it happen. Shae crumpled into the seat as if all of her muscles gave out at once.

"Shae!" Fern shook her by the arms. "Shae!" she shouted again.

CHAPTER EIGHT

Shae blinked. The fleur de lis. The Saints ball cap. The red handkerchief. The man pushed a plastic tray toward her with the sole of his work boot. As it slid, it scraped against the dirt on the floor. Her knee stopped its momentum.

"Eat," he grunted.

She tried to assuage the fear and focus on the details—of the shack, of him—like the detective said. The little bit of hair she could see tucked behind his ears was dark and damp. And there was some scruff rising above the handkerchief, as if he hadn't shaved in a day or two. She took in his height and build and tried to recall Boone's stature but couldn't. The man's fingernails were darkened with dirt and his jeans were stained red on the knees. Not a paint red. She swallowed hard. A *blood* red.

He turned to leave. The door was halfway open. This was her chance.

She wrapped her fingers around the glass of water he'd brought on the tray, emptied it in one quick flick of her wrist, and threw the glass as hard as she could at his head. He fell, probably out of surprise rather than pain, although his hand was cupping his forehead. Apparently, the glass had hit him right above the eye. She ran as fast as she could for the door. He reached for her, grabbing the fabric of her dress. She pulled out of his grasp, leaving a bit of the dress in his hand. She ran out the shack door into the wide open space beyond. It took her eyes a moment to adjust to the sunlight. When they did, she saw open fields on all sides, and it was about a mile to the tree line. She'd never make it that far. But three hundred yards west of the shack was one of those garages that looked like a barn.

The sound of a gunshot behind her made her legs pump harder. She didn't look back. She just ran toward that red barn in the distance. She could hear him yelling something incoherent but clearly angry. He was gaining on her.

The barn was locked with a chain and padlock, but it was just loose enough, *thank god*, to allow her—Alia—to squeeze through. She could hear him outside pulling at the chain.

She scanned the barn. Besides a car covered by a tarp, there were worktables, shelving, boxes, and paint cans. She grabbed the first thing she saw that she might use as a weapon—one of those heavy-duty aluminum straightedge tools. She pulled up the tarp and tried the car door. It was unlocked. She slid inside, locked the doors, and clung to the straightedge as if it were a life preserver.

He was in the barn now. She could hear his movements. She ducked against the passenger side floor, her heart pounding in her ears. When she heard the tarp move against the car, she readied her weapon.

Their eyes met through the window. She could tell he was smiling by the way the handkerchief moved up with his cheeks. He tried the door. *Please don't have the keys. Please don't have the keys.*

He reached into his pocket. He dangled a rabbit's foot keychain in front of the window.

She scrambled to the driver's side and tried to unlock that door. It was too late. He had her foot now. She swung the straightedge like a sword and it sliced his arm open. Blood gushed from the wound onto the ivory seat. She swung again, but he captured the straightedge before it hit him and yanked it out of her grasp. He had her now. His hands wrapped tightly around her ankles. She kicked but it was no use. He pulled her out of the seat and over his shoulder like a sack of meal. She struggled against his grasp, grabbing at anything she could use to pull herself free. She captured the tarp instead of the car. As he carried her toward the door, she looked back at the partially covered car. It was one of those vintage cars with the chrome fender and headlamps, its bluish-green color like the kind decorating tiles in swimming pools. And then everything went black.

Fern was scared. She was driving too fast and she knew it. She'd already run at least one red light and cut off a guy in a Jeep who wasn't afraid to use some pretty obnoxious hand signals to show his irritation.

"Which hospital?" Ruby's voice, tinny through the iPhone speaker, sounded just as panicked as Fern felt.

"St. Charles, I guess. I don't know. Grandma, she's not responding to anything."

She pressed the back of her hand against Shae's cheek. Her skin felt warm. "Shae? Please answer, Shae." Nothing. "What do I do?"

"You're doing it. You take her to St. Charles. I'll meet you there."

"Please hurry."

"I'm on my way," Ruby said and hung up.

Fern glanced at Shae. She hadn't moved. She was in the exact same position Fern had left her in, her legs propped up at the knee leaning against the seat back. Fern had used a balled-up sweater as a cushion between Shae's head and the door. To keep her steady during turns, Fern kept her hand on Shae's side. She was doing that now as she took a sharp turn toward downtown New Orleans. She felt her move.

"What?...Where?" Shae mumbled, pulling herself into a sitting position.

"Shae? Oh my god, Shae!"

Shae's confused eyes met hers. "I made a mistake."

"What?" Fern adjusted the mirror to see her better.

"I made a run for it."

"You were there again?"

Shae nodded, her eyes growing wet with tears. "I tried to get away. It was stupid. Stupid," she said, pounding her fist into her thigh.

Fern veered the car into a Dollar Store parking lot. She put the car in park and turned to face her.

"He's probably going to hurt her for that—for what *I* did." A tear dripped off Shae's chin and fell onto her shirt.

"You don't know that," she said. "You don't even know if it's real."

"I might have just killed her."

Not knowing what to say or do, she took Shae's hand in hers.

"She might be dead because of me," Shae said, studying their clasped hands.

"Do you still have that card the reporter gave us?"

Shae reached into her front pocket and produced a somewhat crinkled business card.

"Good," she said. "Here's what we're going to do." She dug through her purse for her packet of tissues. "We're going to clean you up." She dried Shae's cheeks. "And we're going to see this…" Fern plucked the card from Shae's fingers and read it. "…this Walker woman."

CHAPTER NINE

Elle Walker rubbed her forehead as she stared at the notes on her desk. This was the ninth Alia Ambrois sighting or tip, which, like the other eight, had proven less than accurate. The announcement of a reward made every person a "concerned citizen." When in similar missing persons cases they'd log just a few calls from an overzealous *Law and Order* fan or a frightened parent, the Alia Ambrois hotline was ringing off the hook with people calling in to report all kinds of suspicious activity—a man in a hoodie lingering by a playground or elementary schoolyard, an unmarked van left idling on a neighborhood street or in a grocery store parking lot. Little did the plumbers, repairmen, and floral delivery drivers know that, since the girl's disappearance, they'd been the subject of some frantic calls to the Algiers Point non-emergency police line. Enough calls to make Elle Walker's head pound like a bass drum.

"And what color was the van?" Elle doodled some random shapes on the side of her yellow legal pad. *White again? Just how many white vans with darkened windows can there be in the county?* Readying her pencil, she asked, "Did you happen to get the plate number?" She sighed and wrote "no plate" next to the description of the van. "That's okay. We'll follow up on this right away. Thank you for the information." Elle hung the phone back on its cradle and flipped the page of her notepad. Three more. She wouldn't make it without a couple Ibuprofen.

"This one's for you," a male voice said.

It was a voice she recognized as that of veteran detective Ed Kandinsky, for whom the boys had already thrown a retirement party complete with a graveyard cake and gifts of walkers with mounted side mirrors. He'd all but cleaned out his desk. In fact, the only evidence of him remaining was a framed photo of a woman, probably his wife, holding a beagle dressed in a Hornets basketball jersey, and a desk calendar, each month displaying a different vintage car. It was just like Kandinsky to wait until all the speeches had concluded and all the presents had been opened to announce that he wasn't going to retire after all. That he had one more case left in him. Alia Ambrois. Elle glanced at the phone numbers again. *What she wouldn't give for one solid lead!*

Kandinsky leaned closer and she smelled the stench of stale cigarettes and far too much Old Spice. She wrinkled her nose in response.

"Courtesy of the Chief," he said, dropping a manila file folder on top of her notes. Floating on his words was the noxious smell of his lunch—the same lunch he'd eaten every day she'd known him, despite its power to clear out the break room faster than an agent from Internal Affairs—a tuna fish sandwich on rye. His rank breath was all the motivation she needed to give up sleeping and eating and anything else that took time away from solving the Ambrois case.

She turned to face him then—all six feet and three inches of him. His thick gray mustache grinned at her as he fingered his necktie, a maroon and yellow striped deal that was far too wide for the day's fashion. Playing with the tie was his tell. She'd seen him do it while bluffing with a pair of twos at last Saturday's poker game.

"Yeah right." She pushed the folder off her notes with her elbow, and trying to ignore him, began dialing the next batch of numbers with the eraser end of her pencil.

"Hell, I'll take it if you don't want it," he said, smoothing his tie straight over his puffy man-boob chest with his palm. "A one thirty-two."

Armed robbery? She was lead on a robbery? Excitement rippled through her as she reached for the folder.

"A house in one of those upscale gated communities. The perp broke in through the chimney."

"The what?" she asked, only half listening and rifling through the folder. She scanned the Incident Report's Offenders line: defendant...white male, age sixty-eight, address North Pole. *North Pole?*

"A fat guy in a red suit. Long white beard." Kandinsky could barely get the words out around his laughter. "Left a ransom note. Said something about 'thanks for the cookies.'"

She could hear Kandinsky's partner, Santos, offer a wheezy snicker that reminded her of Dick Dastardly's sidekick, Muttley, in the Hanna-Barbara cartoons of her youth.

"Hysterical," she said drolly, snapping the folder closed with an open palm. "These new detective pranks never get old."

"Ho ho ho!" he chuckled as he made his way back to his desk. In her peripheral vision, she caught Santos high-fiving Kandinsky as he went past.

She closed her eyes and rubbed her temples with her fingers, trying to calm the drum pounding away in her skull.

"Walker!" barked O'Connor, the poor sap whose desk was closest to the precinct's main entrance.

She gritted her teeth in preparation for what was undoubtedly a Kris Kringle jibe.

"Raise your hand so these gals can find you."

What? Elle opened her eyes. Two young women, probably in their early twenties, stood next to O'Connor, scanning the sea of desks with matching focused but anxious expressions. The taller one was a pretty African American girl with an athletic build. No make-up and Chuck Taylor sneakers. Probably a lesbian, Elle thought. The other was a blond blue-eyed beauty, homecoming queen or cheer captain. And based on the designer shoes and expensive looking jewelry she wore, Elle guessed that the girl's parents were the kind with regular tee times and different homes for at least two seasons.

The idea that her coworkers would recruit kids for a prank was unlikely. They were family men at least Monday through Friday—family men to whom the idea of exploiting children would be more than a little distasteful. And they weren't that clever, opting instead to fabricate stories of escaped unicorns and leprechaun bank heists. Given the amount of detail they packed into the narrative and the illustrated mug shots, Elle guessed they got a kick out of writing up the phony police reports.

She waved her hand in the air like an air traffic controller and watched as the girls navigated their way through the rows of desks between her and O'Connor.

"Officer Walker?" homecoming queen asked.

"It's detective now," she said. She tried to tamp down the pride that swelled within her at the mention of the title. "But everyone just calls me Elle. What can I do for you?"

"Madeline Burch sent us."

Maddie? The name jumpstarted her pulse and almost instantaneously spun it into what her piano teacher mother would describe as an *andantino rhythm*. For a moment, she wondered if the girls had a message for her. But then hadn't Maddie said it all already on that last trip to the lake house?

"We're done," she had said, notably looking away from Elle—at the water, which, poetically, was as stagnant as their relationship at the moment. "Done," she repeated. The word folded around Elle's heart like fingers, and squeezed and twisted until all the happiness, all of the love, was wrung out.

She and Maddie had clashed from the start. The woman was insufferable, no sense of humor and demanding as all get out. Before they'd even been officially introduced, Maddie was making demands when she showed up while Elle was taking Boone in for questioning.

"Tell me where you're taking him," she'd said as if talking to a subordinate.

Elle was so surprised she'd forgotten to hold Boone's head as she helped him into the patrol car. He hit it on the doorframe and cursed, causing her to wince in sympathy.

"And who are you?" she asked.

Maddie's strawberry blond hair was cut in a no-nonsense straight style. She pushed some strands behind her right ear as she spoke. "Madeline Burch, with the *Ledger*," she said and pressed the button on a handheld recorder. "Care to comment?"

Maddie wasn't classically beautiful by any means. She had pale skin, freckles, a high forehead, and a slightly upturned nose. The large plastic-frame glasses she wore made her look more like a librarian than a reporter. But to Elle there was something magnetic about her. Her eyes were a bright and deep green like grass in the springtime. Just one look and Elle could conjure the pleasing fresh scent of a recent mow. And she couldn't help but find the woman's obvious inattention to style endearing. Not that Elle had a bold sense of fashion, but Maddie seemed downright allergic to it. It was hard to miss the lumps positioned hanger-width apart in the shoulders of her maroon sweater, a style and color that went with the harem elephant print pants she wore about as well as milk goes with tequila. Spying the woman's tag jutting out from her collar like a fantail, Elle couldn't help but crack a smile.

"What?" Maddie asked.

Elle reached over and gently tucked her tag under her collar—her fingers unintentionally brushing the nape of her neck.

"Oh, thank you. I…" Maddie's cheeks turned a shade of pink that reminded Elle of the rosebushes her grandmother would carefully prune each morning after the first spring frost. If she'd had a little more courage, she would have kissed the woman right then.

"So, officer," Maddie said, moving the recorder closer to Elle's mouth, "Can you tell me why Boone Copeland is handcuffed in the back of your patrol car?"

"It's Elle," she said and took a step closer.

Maddie took a step back. *Were they dancing?* "Elle," she said as if she were trying out the feel of it on her tongue. "Do you... um...have any comment, Elle?"

"I do as a matter of fact."

Maddie seemed to stiffen in response—her expression of amusement replaced now with one that was both driving and steady.

"My comment is," she said, pulling the recorder, and, subsequently Maddie's hand, closer to her lips, "I'd like to take you to dinner."

Maddie pulled her hand back and fumbled with the recorder, obviously looking for the stop button.

"Have dinner with me, Madeline Burch with the *Ledger*."

"Maddie," she said, almost inaudibly.

"Maddie," Elle repeated.

"I need a story, Elle."

"Have dinner with me and you'll have a story."

"About Copeland. I need a story about Boone Copeland."

"It won't be about Copeland but it'll be a good story. I can promise you that."

Maddie snorted. It was a cute, high-pitched sound—a bow on her mismatched outfit, her stretched out sweater and her fantail of a tag. It was official. Elle liked this Madeline Burch—a lot.

And that was how they began. How they ended was not such a nice story.

"And how do you two know Maddie?" she asked the doe-eyed girls.

"We don't...not really," the tall girl said. "We met with her to discuss Alia Ambrois's disappearance."

Not what she was expecting. "What about it?"

The girls exchanged a look that Elle couldn't quite read.

"We think Alia was taken by the same man who took Katie Biggs...Boone Copeland," the homecoming queen said.

Elle blinked. First Maddie with her cover-up stories and now this. "Boone's been cleared in the Biggs case. Besides, who says anyone *took* Katie Biggs?"

"Yes, we know that Boone was cleared. But…"

"But what?" Elle asked.

"But…well…we know…more," the tall girl said.

While Elle's inside voice was reminding her that the girls could be opportunists—maybe a couple of Boone's jilted lovers trying to get even or some money hungry reward chasers—her outside voice was prodding them to continue. "More like what?"

The tall girl's deep brown eyes slid from her desk to the one adjacent to it—where Sanders was interviewing a thug in a skull cap, the perp's knuckles and neck brandishing prison tattoos in faded blue ink. "Can we maybe go somewhere private to talk?" she asked.

The girls didn't look like reward chasers. In fact, given the blonde's Jimmy Choo pumps, her allowance was probably more than Elle's salary. And they didn't look much like spurned girlfriends either. The black one was setting off Elle's gaydar like nobody's business and the longing way she looked at her blond companion made Elle feel sympathetic. Every lesbian falls for a straight friend and it's always devastating. She glanced at the list of phone numbers on her desk and remembered her headache, which had vanished with the girls' appearance. "Follow me," she said and led them to one of the interview rooms.

The girls talked a mile a minute. It was like watching a relay race. As soon as one ran out of steam, the other picked up the baton.

"He had the same dog!" the black girl who'd introduced herself as Shae was saying, her eyes big and round, her volume increasing with her obvious excitement.

"A German shorthaired pointer!" Fern, the blonde, added with matching enthusiasm.

Not much of a smoking gun, Elle thought. Practically every family in a sixty-mile radius had at least one, if not two or three hunting dogs. And the German shorthaired pointer with its webbed feet was an obvious choice for bayou country. Waterfowl was big game around there.

"And the hat. Boone had the same Saints hat as the guy who took Alia. I saw it in his pocket at the bar."

A Saints baseball hat? Well, that narrows it down, Elle thought sarcastically. "You saw the dog and the man wearing this hat chasing Alia?"

The girls exchanged glances and then a mirroring nod, as if some silent decision had passed between them.

"I sort of...I mean...I saw it in a dream," Shae said.

Great! Two crackpots. Elle sighed audibly. "Look," she said, pulling herself erect, and not even trying to hide the irritation from her voice. "I have *actual* leads to follow up on. And wasting a detective's time is—"

"Wait! I can prove it." Shae closed her fingers around Elle's forearm.

Elle slipped back into her seat. *She could at least hear them out.* "Okay then. I'm listening."

Shae was silent for a moment, her eyes scanning the ceiling as if the answer were etched there in the popcorn plaster. "The ponytail holder!" she blurted. "It flew off when he grabbed her. It's probably still there!"

Elle's stomach seized. One pink beaded ponytail holder had been found at the riverbed. Forensics confirmed it to have belonged to the girl. A detail that hadn't been released to the press. *A good guess. It had to be.* "And what did this ponytail holder look like?" she asked.

"It was one of those ones with a ball, like a marble, on the end of the elastic band."

Elle's head was spinning. She felt faint. "What color was it?"

"Pink."

But how could they know? Were they there? Were they involved somehow? Elle placed her hands on the tabletop to steady herself. "I don't know what game you two are playing but—"

"We're not," Shae said. "I swear, we're not." There was something about her expression that made Elle want to believe her.

"Fine. Then, do you mind telling me where you were last Tuesday between two thirty and three thirty in the afternoon?" If they *were* involved somehow, walking into the precinct like this was as good as turning themselves in. As was talking to a reporter. But they still could've seen something. They could've been there.

Shae blinked. "I… I was at work at the Hole in the Wall."

"I assume someone can confirm this?"

She nodded. "Desi, my boss, can. I can give you his number."

Elle pushed a pad and pen toward the girl and turned to the blonde. "And you?"

"I was on my way to my grandmother's house," Fern said, a hint of defensiveness in her voice. "In St. Charles Parish."

"From?"

"New York. Originally, I mean. We were driving from the airport. I'm just here for the summer." She rolled her eyes. "Not by choice of course."

Shae's lips dipped slightly. Elle guessed she didn't want to be reminded that her straight girl crush was leaving in August. *Poor thing.*

"Who was with you in the car?"

"My parents."

"I'll need their numbers too."

While Fern jotted the numbers down, Elle watched Shae. The girl's eyes were glued to her companion's lips, which at the moment were blowing air at a few strands of hair dangling in her face. Elle knew that look. *This girl had it bad.*

Elle doubted that Miss Homecoming Queen and her love-struck lesbian sidekick were directly involved with Alia's disappearance. Of course she'd follow up on their alibis later. Either there was a leak in the department or the girls knew more than they were letting on.

"I'll look into this and be in touch," Elle said. It was the same tired line she'd used to end the phone calls about idling white vans with tinted windows. The same line she'd used the night before to squelch Aunt June's paranoia about her neighbors.

"Why else would he need a shovel at ten o'clock at night?" June had asked in a distinctly nasal whine that matched that of Elle's mother.

"I don't know, Aunt June, but I doubt very much that he's burying dead bodies in his bed of petunias."

"What good is it having a police officer in the family if she won't—"

"I'll look into this and be in touch," she'd said in her practiced, detective tone.

Like June, the girls were appreciative. Shae even reached a hand out for a shake. "I'm so glad we came in to talk to you! To be honest, I didn't think you'd believe us," she said.

Elle took her hand. "I didn't say that I believed you. Yet."

CHAPTER TEN

Since the girls knew about the ponytail holder, Elle was forced to dig deeper into their story—and into Boone Copeland. The Copelands were off-limits, especially to Elle, ever since Maddie had reported on Boone's white glove treatment during the Katie Biggs investigation. Elle wanted to ask the chief for permission to interview the kid about as much as she wanted a root canal.

The chief's blinds were drawn, making her wonder if she should wait for a better time.

"I hear you out there!" he bellowed. *Too late.* "Enter." He seemed genuinely glad to see her. "Walker!" he said in greeting. "I could use a woman's opinion."

Elle cringed. If he asked her about ironing or cooking, she might just deck him.

"Sally's agreed to have dinner with me tonight." He held up two neckties—a navy blue decorated with tiny embroidered golfers and a plaid burgundy. "I want to make a good impression," he said, his eyes big and glassy like those of a puppy dog. Sally was Chief Mike McKinley's soon to be ex-wife and no tie would change that. The only thing holding up the divorce proceedings was that they hadn't yet settled on the custody details of their daughter.

Elle pointed to the burgundy tie, thinking the golfers too whimsical for a custody battle cloaked in a dinner date.

"Yeah, more refined," he said, turning up the collar of his shirt. He fiddled with the tie. "So, what can I do for you?"

"I wanted to talk to you about the Ambrois case."

"What about it?" he asked, pulling the tie's wide end through the knot's loop.

"I've gotten some new information and I'd like to question Boone Copeland."

Without finishing the tightening, he dropped the tie ends and looked up at her. "Boone Copeland has nothing to do with the girl's disappearance."

"That's probably true, but I'd like to question him just the same."

"The department doesn't have the time or the resources for you to jump through rabbit holes that lead nowhere. Drop this thing with Copeland."

"But I—"

"I said drop it."

She swallowed. He'd never been this dismissive with her before. It made her wonder if there wasn't another reason for it. Maybe she'd missed a filing, maybe there'd been a complaint about her.

"And any new information you get on Ambrois goes to Kandinsky. He's lead on the case." McKinley turned his attention back to the tie. "You can go," he said flatly.

She was surprised by the curt tone. He hadn't even asked the reason for her interest in Boone. Clearly, the wounds left from Maddie's article hadn't fully healed yet. Maybe she'd have more luck with Kandinsky. *Yeah, maybe if hell freezes over.*

When Elle arrived at Kandinsky's desk, tuna-breath wasn't there, but the Alia Ambrois files were—right there on his keyboard as if begging her to read them. She glanced around. The neighboring desks were vacant. One o'clock. The guys were probably out to lunch. She managed to ease her pinky finger under the edge of the folder's top before a voice from behind her made her jump.

"Can I help you?"

She jerked her hand back, her heart racing. Santos's forehead was crinkled like an angry accordion.

"I was just looking for some paper to leave Ed a note," she managed.

"About?" There was an edge to his voice that made her worry that if she slipped, it would slice right into her and gut her like a fish.

"I have some news about Boone Copeland. A possible connection to Alia's—"

"I'll be damned if I let you destroy this investigation with your dyke girlfriend's conspiracy theories!" Ed Kandinsky, who had apparently slithered in without her noticing, towered over her now like a great oak, his arms akimbo, a menacing look on his face. "Why don't you leave this to the men, sweetheart?"

Elle gritted her teeth to keep from releasing the "Sexist homophobic pig!" comment itching to get out. "This doesn't involve Maddie," she said instead.

"What's the matter? Did she get tired of your latex dick?" Kandinsky elbowed his partner in the ribs.

"Asshole," Elle said before she could stop herself.

The article had made Maddie Burch and her Boone Copeland obsession infamous at Algiers Point PD. Having your girlfriend challenge the department was a sure way to lose your momentum toward securing the rank of detective. Having a vagina in a male-dominated field was a challenge but being viewed as disloyal was a career ender. She'd told Maddie as much, asking if they could lay low for a while—just a while—until everything blew over. But Maddie was too proud for that.

"How can you side with them?" Maddie had demanded.

"I'm not siding with anyone," Elle explained. "It's my *career*."

"I can see what's important to you now." She turned away. "And what's not," she said just above a whisper.

Elle should have corrected her. Maddie was far more important than the promotion—than her career. She hadn't realized it at the time. But now that she had the title of detective, she understood just how expensive it was. The price was her relationship with Maddie.

Kandinsky's stony expression told her that there was no point in pushing the Boone connection. He wasn't going to budge.

No, if she were going to investigate Boone, it'd have to be on her own, how she pretty much did everything in the days since Maddie left. It had never bothered her before Maddie. She'd never noticed how many things she had done alone— eating alone, waking up alone. She should have recognized it the morning after they'd spent their very first night together, the slight panic that erupted when she'd woken to find cool air rather than warm flesh on her back.

She had listened for the shower. Nothing. She'd dressed quickly, struggling into her jeans, which she'd found crumpled in a pile next to the bed.

"Maddie, you in here?" she asked, flicking on the bathroom light switch. The room was empty—the folded towel she'd left on the vanity untouched. As she made her way around the condo, she could feel herself growing more and more upset by Maddie's absence. No note. No goodbye. *Had it not meant anything to her?*

She practically ran down the stairs. By the fifth step, her nose caught the scent of coffee and something sweet. The panic immediately vanished and was replaced by warmth, by the beginnings of love, only she hadn't known then of course.

"Hey, sleepyhead." Maddie, dressed in nothing but Elle's terrycloth robe, was pouring batter onto a sizzling frying pan. "I hope you like pancakes, Elly." It had always been Elle or Ella, never Elly. But from Maddie's lips, the same lips that had stroked her to climax the night before, the extra syllable felt like a kiss on the end of her name.

"I love pancakes." She wrapped her arms around Maddie's middle.

"Good, because it was either that or Cup o' Noodles. Your pantry doesn't say much about your cooking talents. Or maybe it does."

Elle picked up the box of Bisquick off the counter. "Did you check the date? I didn't even know I had this."

"Well, don't tell me now. I don't want to know."

Elle fiddled with the robe's belt. "I could get used to you cooking for me."

"Pancakes or sex," Maddie said, capturing Elle's hand in hers. "It's one or the other."

"Is that even a choice?"

Maddie laughed. Elle would never tire of her adorable laugh.

Elle stared at Maddie's name in her phone's contact list. She could call her. It had been at least two weeks since she'd left a voice mail. The thought of the last time made her cringe with embarrassment. She'd cried into the phone, blubbered. A whole bottle of cabernet worth of crying and pleading for Maddie to pick up. And then, of course, the pleading turned to anger.

That wasn't the first time. She'd hit rock bottom on Maddie's voice mail more times than she could count. She had unfavorited her name, but she couldn't bring herself to delete the contact. So, there it was—Maddie's cute Facebook photo—a picture that ironically Elle herself had taken on their first vacation together—Maddie peeking up Marilyn Monroe's skirt, or at least a sculpture of Marilyn, in Key West. *God, she wanted to call.* It *was* official business. And maybe a mention of Boone would be enough for Maddie to answer.

* * *

No matter what seats were available, Maddie had always taken the chair directly next to Elle—close enough that Elle believed she could feel the heat radiating off her skin. Seeing Maddie scoot into the booth bench opposite her, instead of the empty seat next to her, made Elle's heart go heavy.

"Hello," she said through tight lips, as if meeting a stranger for the first time.

"How've you been, Maddie?"

"Not as good as you," she said, with an edge of anger. "I heard you made detective." Maddie's eyes were focused on her rolled cutlery. She freed her utensils, breathed on her fork tines, and then wiped them off with her napkin. Madeline Burch was a self-described neat freak, which Elle knew now was an understatement to say the least. The first time they'd stayed at a hotel, a five-star hotel no less, Maddie had brought along a sleep sack. "A hygienic alternative to hotel bedding," she'd explained as if she sold the thing.

Finished with the silverware, Maddie folded her hands in front of her and focused her attention on Elle. "I guess congratulations are in order," she said. Elle searched her face for a hint of sarcasm but found none. Neither did she find a smile. In fact, Maddie's tone and expression were about as emotive as if she were commenting on her sneaker tread instead of Elle's career and the cause of their breakup.

Elle wished they could have celebrated the promotion together—popped some champagne, ordered some take out from that great Thai place in the French Quarter. Maddie had always known how to make her feel special. As it was, getting detective was bittersweet since she didn't have Maddie to share it with.

Maddie dabbed her napkin in her water and brushed at an invisible stain on her sweater. "I have to say I was surprised you called," she said without looking up.

"I don't know why you'd be surprised since I called you practically every day for weeks after you left." Elle couldn't keep the bitterness at bay and Maddie grabbed for her purse. *Damn it. What was she doing?* The last thing she wanted was to make Maddie angrier than she already was. "Look, I'm sorry. I don't want to dredge up the past." Elle blew out a breath.

"Why am I here, Elly?"

Elly. That extra syllable lodged in Elle's chest like a bullet or a dagger. "I called because the girls that I mentioned, they knew something…something we hadn't disclosed to the public. I want to look into their claims about Boone Copeland and I thought you could help."

Maddie's eyes squinted. "What do you need me for when you have an entire police force at your disposal?"

"The lead on the case, Ed Kandinsky, is this jackass who's got one foot out the retirement door and the other wedged into a superhero boot that clearly doesn't fit."

"So?"

"So, he doesn't want my help. Any *woman's* help," she said more to herself than to Maddie. "And—"

"And they're squashing the Boone angle. Again."

"No one's…" Elle remembered the chief's reaction. He hadn't even asked what new evidence she had on the kid. Of course he was probably too caught up in the divorce dinner date to be thinking clearly. "It doesn't matter why it's just me. It is. Will you help or not?"

Maddie looked as if she were a prizefighter sizing up an opponent.

"Maddie, *please?*"

The right corner of Maddie's mouth hitched into a half smile. "I'd do anything to see that guy pay for what he's done," she said. "Yes, I'll help."

The door chimes drew Elle's attention. Fern removed her Dolce and Gabbana sunglasses and hooked them onto her shirt collar. Shae's eyes followed the movement and lingered on Fern's V-neck, lowered slightly by the weight of the glasses. Elle sighed.

"What is it?" Maddie asked.

"The black girl, Shae," she said, waving her hand in the girls' direction. "She's in love with Fern, her straight best friend."

"Really? How can you tell?"

Elle didn't get a chance to answer before Fern scooted into the seat next to Maddie, and the waitress appeared with two menus and place settings.

Fern was so absorbed in the menu that she didn't notice Shae's attention was fixed on her. Maddie must have noticed, though, since she mouthed, "puppy love" to Elle behind the shield of her menu.

The waitress filled the girls' mugs. Elle waited for her to leave before she said, "So, I asked you all here because I think we can help each other. Maddie has a wealth of information on Boone's connections to Biggs and Davis."

"Davis?" Shae asked.

"Rape case," Maddie offered.

"*Statutory* rape," Elle clarified. "Boone was with a sixteen-year-old. He was eighteen at the time. So, there's Biggs, Davis, and now Ambrois. Three black girls." Elle glanced nervously at Shae. "African American."

"I prefer black."

"Why?" Fern asked.

"I'm like four or five generations down the line, Fern. If you sent me to Africa, I'd have no idea how to be. Just like you."

"Black then," Elle said, feeling like the conversation was getting away from her. "So there are two black girls with clear connections to Copeland, a family who bankrolled white supremacist David Duke's senate run. And then there's the Saints hat and the German shorthaired pointer that might connect Copeland to Alia."

"Why don't you just send some cops over to Boone's place?" Fern asked. "I mean, what are we doing here?"

"He's already been cleared in the Biggs case. And my chief… Well, let's just say that he doesn't think it's an avenue worthy of the department resources."

Maddie snorted. "Or he's been paid off like the district attorney."

Here we go again, Elle thought.

"What?" Maddie asked Elle, her arms folded across her chest.

"What what? I didn't say anything."

"You didn't have to. I can see it in your face."

Elle shot Maddie a menacing look. "What's my face saying now?"

Maddie's smile flatlined and she looked away, busying herself with adding some creamer to her tea.

"So, what do you need us for then?" Fern asked.

"I'd like to know more about the…um…dream you say you had, Shae."

Shae glanced around as if expecting the customers at the surrounding tables to be listening in. "So, I was…I mean, Alia was in this shack and—"

"What kind of shack? How big?"

"I don't know, small."

"Like storage shed small?"

"You could maybe fit a queen bed in there, but that's it."

"Ten by twelve? Eight by ten?"

Shae shrugged. "I'm not sure."

"Resin? Steel?"

"Wood. *Old* wood."

"What about the surroundings?"

Shae rolled her napkin into a tight coil. "There's an open field, a line of trees about a mile away, and one of those garages that looks like a barn."

"A car barn?"

Shae nodded. "It was old looking—most of the paint chipped off."

"Did it look like a tobacco barn?"

"A what?" Shae asked.

Elle pulled up a few images on her phone.

"It looks like that with a red roof," she said pointing to one that had a gabled roof, a frame construction, and hinges attached to the cladding boards. *Well, there goes my weekend. I'll spend it driving around the parish looking for a yard with a red-roofed tobacco barn.* "And you saw this barn through the windows in the shack?"

"No, I couldn't see much through the windows. They were pretty grimy."

"How many windows?"

"Two—the kind that push out rather than up."

"Casement windows."

"Could you hear anything?"

The girl unrolled her napkin and ironed it flat with the side of her palm. "No."

"No birds chirping? Running water? Anything?"

Shae shook her head.

"What about the dogs?"

"Dogs?"

"You said that you recognized the dog Boone had as one that was chasing Alia."

"I didn't hear any dogs."

"Probably away from the main residence."

"Well, it's definitely not on the Copeland property," Fern added. "That place is way too manicured for a broken-down shed."

"We don't even know what state it's in." Shae bit the skin on the edge of her thumbnail. "How are we ever going to find her?"

"If he has her," Elle said, "he can take us there himself."

"What? How?" the girls asked in unison.

"He has to go there eventually, right? I mean, he's got to bring her food and—"

"A stakeout!" Maddie practically jumped out of her seat with excitement.

It was during an episode of *Law and Order* that Elle had first learned of Maddie's weird obsession with detective work. She fired question after question about crime scene investigation at Elle, so many questions that they missed the second half of the episode and never found out if the guy was guilty or not.

A couple weeks later Elle and her partner were assigned to stakeout duty for a suspected drug house. When she'd called home to let Maddie know, Maddie practically exploded with excitement. Not fifteen minutes later, Maddie—dressed in all black, carrying a ski mask, an insulated thermos, and an overstuffed backpack—appeared at the station, asking if she could tag along.

"It's not like the movies," Elle had said, studying the tiny birdwatcher binoculars dangling from Maddie's neck.

She looked at Maddie now and could tell her mind was already working on cataloging the stakeout supplies she would bring with her. Last time she'd packed several rolls of duct tape, one of those bleaching powder solutions used to purify water, a freeze-dried meal kit, and glow sticks. She was more prepared for a rave in a third world country than she was for a police stakeout.

Yep, it's going to be a long night.

* * *

Shae had the next day off at the Hole in the Wall, which meant she worked the farm. In addition to the typical animal feedings, the gathering of the eggs, and the tending of the garden, she also had to scrub the animal feeders, rake out the horse stalls, and repair the pig fence. If she could drag herself out of bed at two o'clock instead of five o'clock like normal, she could add some of that to her morning routine. She'd been doing a lot of that since Fern had come back in town, and the exhaustion was starting to catch up with her. *But, hell, it would definitely be worth it to spend the day in a car with Fern.*

"We can take the first shift," she volunteered and then remembered she hadn't even asked Fern what she thought about it. Surely Fern had something much better to do than sit in a car all day with her. "I mean, if you want," she added, looking at her.

"Hell yes, I do."

Misjudging her enthusiasm as sarcasm, she frowned.

"I mean it," Fern said, as if reading her mind. "It'll be fun!"

"Hold on. I don't think you two should—" Walker started.

"They can watch from a distance," Ms. Burch said. "They don't need to *do* anything. And if they see something, they'll call you. Right girls?"

Fern and Shae nodded on cue.

"They're not trained. What if something happens?"

"What's going to happen? They're just sitting in a car."

"We won't do anything, Ms. Walker," Shae said. "We promise."

"Listen, girls, this isn't like the movies. There are bad people out there. And if this Copeland is our guy, he's dangerous."

"We understand," Fern said soberly. "We'll just sit there and watch. And ring you if he's on the move."

The detective shook her head. She was about to protest when Ms. Burch interrupted. "Good, it's settled then. The girls will take the first shift and we'll take the second."

"*We?*"

"I thought you said that stakeouts are never done alone."

The detective stared.

Fern, seemingly playing the part of TV cop, drank down the last bit of her coffee in one dramatic gulp. "Well, let's get going then." And before anyone answered, she was halfway to the door.

Shae had to work to catch up to her. "Listen, Fern, I just have to swing by the house for a bit," she started, thinking that at the very least she had to repair that fence. They couldn't afford to lose a pig. "I can meet you at—"

"I'll go with you."

"What?"

"To the house. It would be good to see your mom."

"I have to do some chores."

"I'll help."

Shae took in Fern's outfit—an expensive looking print blouse and skintight leggings. "Most people don't wear…" *Is that silk?* "…such nice clothes to trim horse hooves and repair the pig pen."

Fern picked up the corner of her blouse in her fingers, inspected it, and then let it fall back onto her stomach. She frowned.

Shae sighed inwardly at the thought that Fern had changed her mind.

"Wait, did you say horses?" Fern asked. If her eyes were any wider, they'd eclipse the diner itself.

So much for relief.

The farmhouse looked more dilapidated to Shae than it had when she'd left that morning. It was as if Fern's proximity brought all of the farm's flaws into focus: the peeling paint, the missing roof shingles, and the leaf-filled rain gutters.

"It needs work," she said as Fern pulled the car to a stop.

"What do you mean? It's great!"

Shae followed Fern's eyes, alight with excitement, to Bessie, their old gray mare, old enough that she couldn't pull the moldboard plow or even a wagon of kids around the field for a joy ride. Bessie was going on twenty-two and had been diagnosed with colic, abdominal discomfort so severe that at times she'd paw and roll in pain. Colic surgery cost anywhere from five to ten thousand dollars, far too much for Shae and her mother to afford. When the pain got bad enough, they'd have to put Bessie down. For now, though, Bessie looked content, too busy grazing to even notice the car, let alone them.

"I'm totally jealous that you have all this!" Fern said.

Jealous? Of this? Shae took in the fields, the stables, the farmhouse, and tried to see it as Fern was seeing it now. But all she could see was what was broken and what was missing. Everywhere she looked, there were needed repairs they couldn't afford and memories of her father that she knew would bring her to tears if she allowed herself to do more than just notice them.

"It's pretty run down," she noted as if she were a home inspector observing the place for the first time. Shae fought a feeling of heartbreak that surfaced at the thought that they'd allowed her father's treasure to decay.

Fern wasn't listening. She was already out of the car and on her way to Bessie. She was walking so fast Shae had to jog to keep up.

"She's beautiful." Fern reached a tentative hand out to the horse but stopped herself before she touched her fur. She looked at Shae questioningly.

"She's as tame as they come." Shae patted the mare's side to demonstrate. Bessie didn't even glance up and just continued munching away, blades of grass dangling from the fur on her face like Christmas tree tinsel.

Fern combed her fingers through the horse's mane. "She's got some gray hair around her eyes."

"She's old," Shae said, "but she's still beautiful. Want to feed her?"

"Yes!" Fern's eyes went wide. "Can I?" she asked, her voice as giddy as a child's.

"Sure, why not? There're some apples in the barn for the kids."

"Kids?"

"The Gallaghers. They have two kids, Micah and Michelle."

"Are they your neighbors?"

"No," Shae said, wishing she hadn't brought them up. "They're our boarders." Shae could see that Fern was confused. "We needed the income," she explained. "After dad…"

"Oh." Fern kicked at a root with her shoe, her eyes fixed on the ground.

"It's actually kind of nice to have them around. And Bill, Mr. Gallagher, he plays a pretty mean harmonica."

Fern flashed an uneasy smile. "It's been hard, hasn't it?"

"What?"

"I just mean it sounds like things have been rough for you and your mom since your dad passed."

Shae nodded. "Yeah," she managed, despite the lump threatening to close her throat.

Fern's fingers laced through her own and squeezed lightly. "I wish I'd been here for you."

"I wish you had too." Shae meant it. She'd missed Fern, although she didn't know just how much until that moment.

They retrieved apples and carrots from the barn and Shae demonstrated how to feed the horse.

"You just stretch your fingers out flat with the treat in the palm of your hand." She had Bessie's attention now. The mare's eyes were fixed to the carrot as if connected by a puppeteer's strings. As she bowed her head to take the carrot, Shae lifted her hand. "When she reaches for it, gently raise your hand toward her mouth, like this." Bessie took the carrot piece and happily munched away. "Now it's your turn."

Fern did just as Shae had instructed and giggled when she felt Bessie's lips on her palm.

"I think she likes you," Shae said. *I do too.*

"Shae! Is that you?" Shae's mother's voice drew their attention to the porch. Camilla stood half inside and outside, straddling the door's threshold, her hand shielding her eyes from the sun in sagging salute.

"Yeah, Mom, it's me." Shae motioned for Fern to follow her.

"Mom, you remember Fern, Ruby's granddaughter," Shae said as she took the final step onto the porch.

"Of course I do!" Her mother took Fern into her arms for one of her quintessential Camilla hugs that earned her the nickname C-bear. Shae's dad was the one to anoint her C-bear after some Cornelius bear from a comic strip. It was a fitting name since Camilla's hugs made Shae feel as if she was being swallowed whole in a comfy sweater or wrapped in a cushy down comforter. She could tell Fern felt that way too since she looked just a little embarrassed but warm and happy, nonetheless.

"So what have you been up to, Fernanda. How do you like New York? Have you been to the Statue of Liberty? What does that 9-11 Memorial look like up close?" There was no time for Fern to answer a single question. As soon as she opened her mouth to respond, another was on its way. "Oh, and Fifth Avenue. Is it as glitzy as they say?"

"Mom, how about you give her a second to answer?"

"Oh, I'm sorry." Camilla looked embarrassed. "It's just been so long."

"Actually, I was kind of enjoying all the attention." Fern smiled. "So, in answer to your question, I like New York. It's a lot busier than here, which can be annoying when you're trying to get somewhere fast, but it more than compensates in museums and restaurants. I have been to the Statue of Liberty, although I haven't gone inside since it's always under construction."

Fern paused. "The 9-11 Memorial is heartbreaking, but it's also beautiful. All the names..." Fern's voice grew soft. "It's overwhelming."

"Yes, I imagine it is," Camilla said. Everyone grew silent. "So, on a happier note, Ruby tells me you're at Syracuse?"

"Yes, I'm studying aquatic biology."

"Impressive. Your parents must be very proud."

"I guess," Fern shrugged. "I think Dad wanted me to go to Duke, his alma mater."

"Well, Syracuse, that's a very good school. Isn't it, Shae?"

She asked this as if Shae were an authority on the subject—as if Shae could rattle off the top college and university rankings like she could the contents of each aisle in the feed store. "It's a great school," she said, feigning enthusiasm. Even though she liked that her mother was praising Fern, she wished they could talk about something other than college. It made her feel uncomfortable. *It makes me feel less than Fern.*

"Stunning *and* smart! I bet the boys are practically killing each other to get your attention."

My mistake. Let's go back to talking about colleges.

"I, well... " Fern's eyes bounced from Camilla to Shae. It was a pleading look, one that said, *Please get me out of this.*

"She doesn't want to talk about her boyfriends, Mom."

"What girl doesn't want to talk about her boyfriends?" Camilla must have realized her gaffe partway through the sentence because *friends* fell off and was nearly inaudible. At the same time her smile faded. "I did it again, didn't I?" she said, looking particularly apologetic.

"It's no big deal," Shae said.

"I'm sorry, honey."

Shae loved that her mother cared enough about her to monitor her language. "It's okay, Mom."

"No, it's not okay. I should have said, 'What girl doesn't want to talk about her *partners?*' Right? Is that right?"

Shae nodded, despite the fact that she never liked the word *partner*—too business sounding. It made her think of women in blazers and heels in a boardroom clicking through PowerPoint slides or fiddling with the phone for a conference call. She said none of that, though. She didn't want to discourage her mother's evolution—inclusive language *was* a step in the right direction.

"I shouldn't have even assumed that you were straight, Fern. Gosh, I've got so much growing to do." Camilla frowned. "Are you straight, Fern?"

"*Mom!*" Shae was mortified. She couldn't believe Camilla had asked that. Judging by Fern's newly rosy hue, she couldn't either.

"What?" her mother asked, genuine surprise on her face.

"You can't just ask people that."

"Why not? Weren't you the one talking about heterosexual privilege? The fact that we all just assume?"

"Yes, but—"

"I'm just correcting my assumption."

"And I appreciate that, Mom. It's just…for some people it's personal."

"Well, I'm sorry, Fern," Camilla said. "It seems I can't say anything right."

"It's okay, Mrs. Williams. And I think it's great that you're so cool with Shae's sexuality."

"See that, Shae? Fernanda thinks I'm cool."

"You are cool, Mom," Shae said and kissed her mother's cheek.

Camilla smiled. "Why don't you girls come in and I'll use my coolness to fix you something to eat?"

"Thanks but I've got to get that fence repaired."

"Now? But you have company?"

"We have plans today. That's why I'm here. I want to get the fence done before we leave."

"Plans?" Her mother looked from Shae to Fern, her eyebrows raised.

"We're—"

"We have a date," Fern said and swung an arm around Shae's shoulder.

Shae was dumbstruck. *Did she just say date?*

Camilla's polite smile turned genuine then, as evidenced by the deep crows' feet that appeared at the corners of eyes. "Oh my gosh! I'm so happy for you two! And here I'm blathering on about boyfriends..."

Shae was too stunned to speak.

"Thanks," Fern said. With a tug of her arm, she spun Shae around. "So, let's get to that fence then."

CHAPTER ELEVEN

Fern pushed her sleeves up to her elbows.

"You sure you don't want something else to wear? That's a pretty blouse," Shae said. "It'd be a shame to ruin it."

She glanced at her outfit. It *was* a nice blouse—a hundred-fifty on sale at Neiman Marcus.

Shae motioned to a hooded sweatshirt hanging from a peg on the wall of the barn. "It's clean. I swear."

Truthfully, she didn't want to get dirty. She just didn't want to seem like a priss. But Shae didn't appear to be judging her. She pulled her blouse over her head. When she'd freed her eyes from the fabric, she caught Shae looking at her. She knew that look. It was the same look she'd seen on the boys' faces when they'd watched the girls' swim team compete. Within a second, though, Shae had turned away leaving her to wonder if she hadn't imagined it.

She struggled into the sweatshirt as quickly as she could. "You can turn around now," she said when she had the potato sack-size sweatshirt straightened on her shoulders. She took in her new pear-like shape. *Could there be anything less flattering?*

Shae turned back but her eyes didn't. They remained fixed to the floor.

"What do you think?"

"Of what?"

"Me in my new sweatshirt dress?" She curtsied with the ends of the fabric stretched wide in her fingers.

Shae glanced up. A smile lingered on her lips as her gaze scanned Fern from ankle to neckline. She felt warm everywhere Shae's eyes touched her.

"I think you might just start a fashion trend," Shae said.

"I'll take that as a compliment."

She needn't have changed. She wasn't going to get dirty performing the very important job of holding the supplies while Shae worked to repair the chain-link fence. She would have liked to have done more, but Shae was adamant about needing her to hold the wire cutters, the roll of mesh wire, and some big metal T-shaped thing while she worked to remove the damaged section of fence by unwinding it with pliers.

"Shae?"

"Yeah?" she asked, weaving a section of new mesh into the remaining fence.

"What's it like?"

"What's what like?"

"You know...being with a girl?"

"Shit," Shae said, dropping the pliers.

Fern leaned down to retrieve them and they bumped heads on their way back up.

"Ow."

"Sorry."

"My fault."

Shae turned her attention back to the fence. "Can you hand me the fence puller?"

"I'm assuming that's this big thing." Fern picked up the T-shaped metal tool.

"That's it." Shae attached the tool by sliding its bar through the mesh. Then she cranked the tension bar. "Why did you tell my mom that we were going on a date?"

"I don't know. I just figured she'd be more likely to let you go on a date with me than she would a stakeout of a potential murderer."

"True," Shae laughed, "but now we have to come up with a reason to break up."

"Why do we have to break up? We just started dating."

"Trust me. You don't want Camilla to get her hopes up." Shae reattached the tension bar to the band and released the fence puller. "So, I didn't want to have to say this, but... Well, it's not you. It's me."

"Oh no, you're not breaking up with me like that."

"I'm not?"

"No, you're not. At least have the decency to wait until after we've spent the entire day in a car together."

"Good point." Shae smiled. "So, we'll hold off ending it until tonight then."

"That puts a bit of a damper on the afternoon, don't you think?"

Shae laughed. "We'll just have to try not to think about it."

And she tried not to think about it. Even though her brain knew that Fern had made the dating comment just to save her mother some worry, her heart coddled the words, just as they had the memory of Fern blowing the seeds off that dandelion flower when they were young.

As Elle had instructed, they sat and watched—watched the gardener trim the hedges, an older man in a golf cart disappear up a hill in the backyard, the Fed Ex and postal carriers deliver mail and several packages, and the sanitation crew pick up the recycling. But no Boone.

The more time that passed, the smaller the Prius felt to Shae.

"How's your community college class?" she asked, propping her feet on the dashboard in an attempt to get comfortable.

"Have you seen that show with Chevy Chase? *Community?*"
Fern laughed. "It's like that."

Shae had seen the show and she didn't care for it, mostly
because it made it seem like community college was a joke. Her
father had taken night classes in accounting at the community
college so that he could make sense out of the farming contracts
he was offered. She saw how hard he had worked, how seriously
he had approached his studies, sometimes reading into the early
morning hours before heading off to the fields without any
sleep. "Dad went to community college."

Fern's smile melted. She looked apologetic or embarrassed,
Shae wasn't sure which. "I didn't mean…"

"I know what you meant. You go to Syracuse." What
she wouldn't give to go to Syracuse. "But honestly, Fern,
sometimes you sound like you think that everyone has the same
opportunities."

"You're right."

"Hell, I don't even have the money to go to a community
college. Which, by the way, I'd love to do!" She stopped, her
brain suddenly making sense of Fern's words. "Wait, what did
you just say?"

"I said, you're right." Her gaze was fixed on the seat cushion.
She swallowed. "I am fortunate. I mean, I know I've had it way
easier…than you."

Fern's admission melted her irritation. "Well, then," she
said, "I expect you to throw me a solid gold door knocker or
two when you hit it big."

"That might hurt. If it's solid and all."

"Oh, you're funny, Fern. Really funny."

"You love it."

"I do," Shae said and meant it.

They both perked up when they heard a dog barking. Out
came Boone's dog, Bella, racing as if she were a young greyhound
following a mechanical rabbit. She ran the front yard in two
wide circles before slowing down to sniff for the perfect spot to
do her business.

"When did you know?" Fern asked, obviously losing interest in the dog.

"Know what?"

"That you were, you know, gay, or lesbian, or whatever."

Here we go. "I'm not really sure. I mean, I guess I always knew."

"You knew when you and I—?"

"Oh, no, not when I was that little. I mean I had innocent crushes on girls but I didn't know what they were…not then."

"Crushes? Like on who?"

Shae swallowed hard. "I can't remember that far back."

Fern looked unconvinced. "So when did you *really* know?"

"Probably the same time you started to think about boys."

Fern started folding a receipt into smaller and smaller squares. "Why do you like girls better?"

"That's a weird question."

"Is it?" Her eyes were on the paper square—now too small to fold again.

"I didn't have a choice. People are born gay. They don't just decide to like one gender over the other."

Fern looked down, embarrassed.

"But, to answer your question, what I like about women is their strength, their intelligence, their humor, their friendship, their loyalty, their curves, their…" Shae looked at her lips, the bottom one wedged between her teeth. "Their lips."

Fern's lips were moving now, and Shae forced herself to look away. "Every woman's lips?" she asked.

Shae dragged her gaze back.

"What about mine?" Shae's mouth went dry as Fern wet her lips with her tongue.

Was she imagining it or was Fern flirting with her? "What do you mean?"

"If I were gay, what would you think of me?" Fern pushed a fallen hair behind her ear.

Shae's face heated. "I think you're beautiful."

Fern smiled. "I bet you have a lot of girlfriends."

"Why?"

"Women probably think you're...attractive."

Do you think that?

"Do you...have a lot of girlfriends, Shae?"

Shae shook her head.

"Why not?"

"Guess I haven't found what I'm looking for yet."

Was she imagining it or was Fern leaning closer?

"What is it you're looking for?"

She was definitely leaning closer. They were so close that Shae could almost feel Fern's breath heating her skin. And she didn't need any more heat. Her body was like molten lava despite the steady stream of air-conditioning. She could feel a trickle of sweat drip down her back.

Shae thought of the upside down Hanged Man card on Lilith's table. Were her feelings about Fern the thing she was supposed to learn, the lesson that she had been avoiding? "I maybe had...a crush on you," she whispered. "When we were little." It was out. She couldn't take it back now. Shae closed her eyes, not wanting to see Fern's expression. *Would she be disgusted?* "I can't believe I said that out loud."

She felt Fern's fingers close around her right thigh. When she opened her eyes again, Fern was staring at her, the blue of her irises dark like deep, stormy oceans. And like those poor sailors lured by the Sirens' enchanted music to shipwreck on the rocky shores, Shae moved closer still. Her brain wasn't working. She couldn't think past the softness of Fern's lips, now moist from her tongue. She was just about to press her lips to Fern's when a noise at the driver's side window made her jump.

It was the detective, hitting her metal flashlight against the fogged up glass and motioning for her to lower the window.

"Anything?" Walker asked.

"No, not so far." Shae's voice cracked. She moved back—away from Fern—toward her side of the car. She needed to get control of herself.

The detective's gaze passed from Shae to Fern and back to Shae again, her lips creasing into a knowing smile.

"Well," she said, with a jovial tone in her voice that made Shae want to crawl under the seat and hide. "You girls probably have…other things to do. You can go on home now. I appreciate the time you've spent. Maddie and I will take it from here."

Shae glanced around for Ms. Burch and saw a hand wave in the Chevy idling behind them.

"You'll let us know if anything exciting happens?" Fern asked.

"I promise." The detective leaned in through the open window. "And you do the same," she whispered in Shae's ear.

They hadn't spoken since Elle Walker had interrupted… well, whatever that was…and they weren't talking now, except for the, "Oh sorry," that Shae muttered when they'd bumped hands, Shae shifting gears and Fern reaching for her Pepsi in the center console. Fern felt confused about what had happened— more so about what hadn't happened but almost did. She had wanted Shae to kiss her. She was flirting with her, for god's sake! Flirting with a girl. As they drove in silence, Fern's brain was busily cataloging all of the close relationships she'd had with girls—analyzing them—looking for anything that might explain this.

Zoe, her college roommate, and she might as well have been Siamese twins since they spent so much time together. They ate together, took classes together, went on double dates together, and even occasionally slept in the same bed together. But she had never wondered what Zoe's lips felt like—*not once*. In fact, she'd never even noticed her lips except when comparing lipstick shades and considering whether she should borrow Zoe's for a new outfit. And Zoe was pretty—really pretty—with long blond hair and sun-kissed freckled cheeks. A Londoner, she had a totally irresistible British accent that made her jokes seem wittier and her speech sound smarter. But a look from Zoe had never caused goose bumps to flare on Fern's skin the way Shae's had when Fern had caught her staring while she changed in the barn. One of Zoe's innocent touches had never flooded

Fern's body with warmth the way Shae's had when she'd hugged her in the car on the way home from the Hole in the Wall.

She thought back to her experiences with boys like skating the couples' skate with Scott Harris, with Lady Antebellum's "Need You Now" playing in the background, their sweaty hands awkwardly clinging to each other. Fern felt all those uncomfortably insecure but wonderfully gooey feelings that twelve-year-olds feel and don't entirely understand. And the excitement she felt at sixteen when she let Jim Garcia cop a feel behind the bleachers after the track meet, his wet, sloppy kisses tasting of the peach schnapps he'd stolen from his parents' liquor cabinet. She'd enjoyed it with boys. So she couldn't be gay.

As if her memories were mocking her, Nicole Granger—with all of her adorable fourteen-year-old bravado—suddenly appeared—the right side of her uniform pants showing evidence of that awesome slide into home plate she'd made in the final inning of the championship game.

Nicole was a year ahead of Fern in school, and seventh and eighth graders didn't typically fraternize. Rarely did they get opportunities to do so, except during the annual pep rallies or school plays. There was something about Nicole, though, some unique strength, some boyish charm that made Fern desperate to befriend her. Of course, she was too scared to talk to her, but she remembered lying awake at night and dreaming up conversations they would never have. Despite the fact that she didn't ever miss one of her games, they hadn't officially met—at least not until that sunny day in early May.

It was unusually hot and humid that day, and Fern could still remember the way the thin cotton material of her T-shirt clung to her body like an extra skin.

The game had just ended and they had won four to two. Fern was making her way toward the exit, along with all of the other spectators, students and parents, when she spied a garbage can by the restroom. She veered off from the crowd to get rid of the empty soda can she was carrying and almost collided with Nicole, who was just leaving the girls' locker room.

"Fern, right?"

Unable to speak, Fern nodded.

"I'm Nicole, but everyone calls me Nick." She extended her hand for a shake.

Fern took her hand and felt her body explode with nervousness.

"I've seen you here at all the games."

"Yeah?" *She noticed me. She actually noticed me!*

"Do you play?"

Fern shook her head. Her mind was reeling so quickly that she couldn't catch any actual words that would make sense together. So even though Nicole appeared to be waiting for her to say something, she remained silent and just blinked with an especially silly grin plastered on her face.

"Those are cool sneakers," Nicole finally said.

She stared at her Chuck Taylors. She had drawn nonsensical squiggles and geometric shapes all over them in different colored markers. "Are you making fun of me?" she asked, suddenly self-conscious.

"No. I mean it." Nicole smiled, revealing an adorable dimple in her left cheek. "I've seen your drawings on the wall in the art room."

She blushed furiously.

"You're really good."

"Thanks," she said to the ground.

Out of the corner of her eye, she caught a glimpse of some of Nicole's teammates walking toward them; the sight of them prompted an irrational fear to rip through her like lightning.

"Well, it was really nice meeting you, Fern," Nick said. "Next Saturday, sit towards left field. I'll try to hit one that way."

"Okay," Fern said beaming.

Nicole did hit one into the stands near Fern's bleacher the following Saturday. And she winked at her as she rounded second. Fern could remember feeling at that moment like she was the luckiest girl alive. She didn't see much more of Nick after the season ended since she went off to high school and Fern still had eighth grade to suffer through. By the time she was finally a freshman, Nicole was gone, her father's job transferring him to the West Coast.

Because of her compliment, she wore those Chuck Taylors way past their time, cramping her toes to fit into the too-small footbed. And she remembered staying up nights to dwell in secret on the details of their little May exchange. Although she didn't know it then, it was painfully obvious to her now that she had had a crush on Nicole Granger. It wasn't sexual, or at least nothing of that nature had crossed her inexperienced thirteen-year-old mind. But what if Nicole and Fern had been a little older—a little worldlier? Might something have happened between them?

And then she remembered the beautiful Beth Knight who sat two seats to her right in biology the previous semester. It was a mass lecture so people could sit wherever they wanted, but Beth always sat in the same seat—next to Fern.

"Is this seat taken?" she had asked on that first day.

"Nope."

She slung her backpack over the back of the auditorium seat. "Hey, you're Fern, right?" she asked.

"Yeah, how'd you know?"

"I'm Jessie's roommate, Beth." Beth had sapphire blue eyes made even more striking by her chocolate brown hair and brows. Her long hair curled into flawless ringlets, and she was dressed in some sort of cross between indie and vintage styles. Fern liked the way she looked.

"Oh, well, hi," Fern said, taking her hand.

While Dr. Cooper rattled on about the stages of mitosis and she added legs and feet to the mitochondria she had doodled in her notebook, Beth leaned over and whispered, "Do you think that's his real hair?"

She eyed the professor. The hair around his ears was white but the hair on top of his head was an unnatural shade of reddish orange—like burnt cheese. It seemed thicker and she imagined that it was a different texture.

"I think it's road kill—maybe a fox," she said.

Beth laughed. And that laugh began their friendship.

Beth and Fern often went out to frat parties together, especially when Zoe was occupied with her new graduate school boyfriend, Zach. On one particular night, they had had far too much to drink and a couple cute guys convinced them to play spin the bottle.

Fern remembered Beth was interested in Kevin, this guy sitting to Fern's left. Beth gave the bottle a pretty good spin, but it passed Kevin and settled on Fern. The guys whistled and started chanting "Kiss her! Kiss her!" Beth didn't look the slightest bit nervous as she crossed the room and made her way toward Fern. She pushed some of Fern's fallen hair behind her ear with her fingers and pressed her soft lips against Fern's. Fern remembered feeling her tongue slide along her bottom lip for just a second before she released her. When she stepped back, everyone clapped and hooted. Beth smiled at her. It was a strange smile, a secretive smile. She remembered liking the kiss, even wanting it to continue longer than it did. But she had dismissed that feeling as nothing more than the buzz from the alcohol and the excitement of the game.

She thought of the warmth that filled her as she'd watched Shae work on the fence—the light mist of perspiration dotting Shae's neck and shoulders, making her cocoa-colored skin glisten in the sunlight. The muscle definition in her arms made even more visible by her straining with the pliers. Fern couldn't help but ask it. "What's it like to be with a girl?" It was a stupid question, she knew. Even a dangerous question. But she'd wanted to know. She'd wanted to hear Shae describe it to her. If she was honest with herself, she'd say that she wanted to know what it would be like to be with Shae.

"Listen, Fern, we should probably talk about what happened," Shae said now, breaking the silence.

Fern couldn't look at her. Instead she watched the little shotgun houses go by like railroad cars. *Could she be bi and not have known? What would her parents say? What would her friends say?*

"Did something happen?" Fern regretted it before she'd even finished asking the question.

"I thought—" Shae stopped. "Nothing. Forget it."

They drove the rest of the way in silence while Fern thought of all the things she wished she'd said instead.

CHAPTER TWELVE

When Elle slid into the driver's seat, she found that Maddie had already made herself comfortable. Her bare feet were propped on the dashboard of Elle's new Silverado. "I hope your feet are clean."

"Of course they're clean."

Elle wasn't so sure, remembering how Maddie used to slip out of her shoes practically every chance she got—her feet aching after spending any amount of time in shoes with even a slight heel. Elle used to massage Maddie's achy feet as they watched television together on the couch. "Well, just don't dirty up my dash."

Maddie walked her way from the dash to the windshield and pressed both feet flatly against the glass.

"Oh, that's nice."

Maddie laughed. "I thought *I* was the clean freak."

"Not when it comes to your feet." Spying something green on her dashboard, she asked, "Is that grass?"

Maddie rolled her eyes.

Elle reached over Maddie to open her glove compartment, to look for a tissue or napkin she could use to return her truck to its pristine pre-Maddie invasion state. A Snickers bar tumbled out. She managed to catch it before it fell into Maddie's lap.

"Still eating healthy I see."

"Always." Elle scooped up the candy bar, and knowing that it would make Maddie, the germaphobe, cringe, she ripped the wrapper open with her teeth. "Want some?"

"No thanks. I'll pass on the corn syrup solids and food coloring."

Elle swallowed her first bite of chocolaty, caramel goodness. "Your loss," she said.

"Your gain." Maddie poked her stomach.

Elle glanced down. "What? I eat my feelings."

"And what feelings are those exactly?"

What feelings are those? Hadn't she heard those feelings in the zillion voice mails Elle had left for her? It was true. She had eaten her way from a size eight to a size ten since the day Maddie had left. She didn't want to get into it. Not now. "Any feelings, doesn't matter. I'm not picky. I'll eat 'em all."

Maddie smiled. "Well, it looks good on you."

"What?" She let out a breath and allowed her stomach muscles to relax. Even the tens were snug now. "Sorrow looks good on me?" A noise redirected her attention to the house.

"Who's that?" Maddie asked.

"That," Elle said, struggling to position her binoculars, "is Boone Copeland."

"What's he doing just standing there?"

Elle peered through the binocular lenses. "He's waiting for something." She squinted through the glass and watched as he turned his wrist several times, his foot tapping out a maniacal rhythm of impatience. They heard it before they saw it—the purr of an engine belonging to a car that cost more than Elle's house. And sure enough, a cherry red Aston-Martin Vanquish appeared at the top of the hill in the driveway as if by magic. It had presumably come from the Copeland's car library in the back of the residence. Copeland Senior had described it that way in an interview—not a pedestrian, common *garage* but a car *library* with porcelain floors and cherry wood walls, and most importantly, a collection of very expensive cars.

The valet pulled the sports car to a stop in front of Boone. He exited the vehicle and held the door open for Boone. He slid into the leather seat and swung the door closed behind him without even a thank-you or a nod of acknowledgment.

Elle watched the Aston-Martin exit the property and travel west. She maintained a good distance but kept her eyes fixed to that candy red bumper. He drove through neighborhood streets onto Highway Business 90 West. He continued for several miles before turning off on an exit ramp. They followed him past boat docks and parks until he turned down a dirt road that ran parallel to the river. Elle cut the lights and continued at a crawl. She spotted the car first—its lights extinguished and its seats empty. Boone was out of the vehicle and walking toward the river.

"What's he doing?" Maddie whispered.

"I don't know." It was dark, the only light coming from the reflection of the crescent moon and the stars on the water. And there was nothing there, nothing except the river, trees and underbrush. Elle squinted through her binoculars. *What is he doing here?*

"I can't see much of anything," Maddie said.

"Me neither." All she could make out was Boone kneeling by the riverbed—kneeling as if he were praying. After a few moments, he stood, brushed at his knees and headed back to the car. Elle waited for the lights of the Aston-Martin to disappear before heading out to investigate.

"We're going to lose him."

"We are," Elle said, grabbing a flashlight from the glove compartment. "You stay here." The last thing she needed was Maddie slipping on some mud and hurting herself.

"This isn't like one of those horror movies where the blonde gets hacked to pieces while the boyfriend investigates, is it?"

"Well, you have nothing to worry about then, Ginger." She winked.

"Just be quick about it." Elle could tell by the staccato words and the strain in her voice that Maddie was genuinely nervous.

"It'll be okay," she said, to reassure her.

She made her way to the riverbed where Boone had knelt, her senses on high alert for any indication that he was on his way back.

There was nothing in the water but some floating swamp grass and bubbles from either decomposing algae or a passing school of fish. She could see where he'd knelt because there were two shallow depressions in the grass. As she scanned that area with her flashlight, something sparkled. Brushing some grass away with her hands, she uncovered it—a gold necklace—far too small for any adult woman's neck. On its end hung a ladybug pendant, three black dots on each red wing and gold legs curling out from its sides at odd angles as if frozen mid-climb. It was undoubtedly a child's necklace. A chill ran up her spine. Since she didn't have gloves, she dug in her pocket for something she could use to pick it up and found a pen.

"What is it?" Maddie asked when Elle returned to the car.

"A necklace." She held it out for Maddie to see.

"My god!" she said. "That could be Alia's. Is it some sort of trophy?" Maddie cupped her mouth with her hands as if shocked by her own thought.

Elle shook her head. "I doubt it. A trophy is something a criminal keeps, prolonging the fantasy of the crime. If it is a trophy, he wouldn't leave it here. He would keep it. It doesn't make sense."

"Murdering little girls doesn't make sense, so maybe that's not the right yardstick to use to measure this guy's actions."

Elle understood where Maddie was coming from, of course, but she also knew from her work with profilers that, however deranged a serial killer might be, there was some method to his madness. She just had to figure out Boone's. That meant looking back through the Katie Biggs case file and interviewing some of his friends.

* * *

Elle felt no closer to an answer after having spent the better part of the afternoon riffling through evidence boxes and files from the Biggs case. Naming Copeland a person of interest was a stretch. If not for a neighbor's account of having seen him on the property a month prior to Katie's disappearance, there'd be nothing linking him to the Biggs family. Calvin Wright, the elderly man who lived behind the Biggs', had reported seeing Boone at a back bedroom window on the property. "I have trouble sleeping, you see," he said in the interview transcript, "so I was up watching the *Late Show* and having a nightcap when I saw the light. I wouldn't have been able to see him if it weren't for the fact that he had his flashlight angled that way."

"Angled how?" asked Detective Donnely, who interviewed Mr. Wright.

"Sort of up. I guess so's he could see the window lock. I couldn't see what he was doing, but it sure looked like he was trying to break in."

"And you know it was Boone Copeland?"

"I knew him right away. Seen 'em on the news—the Copeland Charity Ball and all."

When asked why he didn't call the police, he said, "A clean-cut white boy breaking in to a house here? No one would've believed me." He was right, of course. The prospect of Boone's presence in this neighborhood, a USDA *Black high poverty parish*, was more than suspicious.

But a movie ticket stub and an Instagram photo placed Boone at a party on the date and time Mr. Wright claimed to have seen him. At the time, Elle had chalked the eyewitness account up to too many nightcaps. But now, with the necklace, she wondered if she should have taken it more seriously.

The necklace wasn't Alia's. She'd ruled that out that morning.

She'd known almost immediately by the relief that set in Mr. Ambrois's expression when she'd placed the charm on the coffee table in front of him and his wife.

"Oh, thank god," he'd said, staring at the little ladybug on the glass. He patted his damp brow with a handkerchief. Mrs. Ambrois opened her eyes then.

"It's not hers?" Elle asked, watching Mrs. Ambrois let out a breath that said more to Elle than any words could.

"She never liked insects," Mr. Ambrois said. "Her brother put fake ants in the girls' sleeping bags at her birthday party." He patted his brow again. "You would've thought they were live snakes judging by how much she screamed and carried on."

Elle couldn't shake the image of Mrs. Ambrois with her eyes squeezed shut, probably praying that whatever thing Elle was going to show her—a bit of fabric, some hair found in a branch, a shoe—wouldn't rid her of the hope that her daughter was still alive.

As Elle made her way up the Biggs's driveway, she was thinking about that—all the things that must have been going through Mrs. Ambrois's mind as she waited for some sign from her husband, telling her that it was safe to look. Elle was so wrapped up in her thoughts that she didn't notice the dog.

It lunged at her, making her heart leap into her throat. She almost fell backward as she scrambled to get away from it. Before it could clamp its teeth around her leg, it was stopped short by the length of a thick chain that extended to a metal loop cemented into a concrete slab. The choker collar had little effect on the dog's bark, though, which was ferocious enough to cause Elle to walk on the grass rather than the concrete. Cujo continued to lunge, each time choking itself on its collar and chain.

The Biggs's home was a small rectangular shotgun house, with clapboard siding in need of repair and floor-to ceiling-shutters with missing slats. An old wicker love seat, the cushions water-stained and faded, sat against the wall of the house on what she guessed was once a porch but was now little more than a tattered screen stapled to rotting boards. As soon as she stepped onto the porch, she heard voices.

"I babysat for June all day on Friday!" a teenage girl said, judging by the whiny lilt. The voice grew louder as the girl got closer to the door. "I'm not about to give up my Saturday because my cousin doesn't know how to use birth control!"

"You get back here, young lady!"

Elle stepped back just in time to avoid being hit by the screen door. A tall, lanky black girl a little older than she sounded rushed past her like a tornado.

And then came the mother. "We didn't raise you to talk about your family like—"

The woman stopped short when she spotted Elle. Her hand, which had been waving a spatula in the air as if it were some kind of medieval weapon, froze mid-swing.

"Mrs. Biggs, I'm Detective Walker with Algiers Point PD." Elle flipped her leather badge case open and held it out for the woman to inspect.

She barely glanced at it and instead exclaimed, "Have you found something? Is this about Katie?" She dropped the spatula on the stoop and stared at Elle through big white eyes.

"No ma'am. I just have a few questions for you. If you have a moment, it would help with the investigation."

"Investigation? I thought you all closed the investigation?"

Elle bit her bottom lip. It was a poor choice of words. The case had been closed with the medical examiner's ruling that Katie's death was an accidental drowning. "No homicide, no investigation," the chief had said, removing the crime scene photos from the investigation room corkboard.

The coroner's report may have been enough for the chief, but it wasn't enough to convince Maddie. Elle guessed that nothing short of an interview with the deceased girl herself would put the case to rest in Madeline Burch's mind.

"Yes, you're right, Mrs. Biggs," she said now. "I'm just following up on something. It may not even be related to your daughter's case, but I just want to be sure."

Elle heard a car door slam behind her. She resisted the temptation to turn and look.

"You be back here by nightfall!" Mrs. Biggs yelled in the car's direction.

"Whatever!" the girl yelled back and cranked up the volume of her car stereo. The bass was so loud Elle thought she could feel her fillings in her mouth shake.

The car peeled out of the driveway.

"It's the age," Mrs. Biggs said, her eyes on the spatula.

Elle bent to retrieve it. "A conversation with my fourteen-year-old niece feels a little like walking through landmines, so I get it."

Mrs. Biggs laughed and took the spatula from Elle's hand. "Come in," she said, and held the screen door open with her hip.

The Biggs's kitchen was cluttered. There was barely any countertop visible what with the stacked Tupperware, appliances, knife block, bag of flour, boxes of tea, cup of pens, and a basket of those little packets of soy sauce and ketchup from take-out orders. An open textbook suggested the island doubled as a work or study space. A desk fan cycling back and forth made the photographs and kids' drawings affixed to the refrigerator flutter in the breeze like streamers at a parade.

"That's Katie's."

"What?" Elle asked, confused.

Mrs. Biggs motioned to a coloring book page fixed to the fridge with an *Obama: Made in the USA* magnet. The page featured a rabbit with rainbow crayon stripes that extended past the lines. Elle smiled and then immediately wondered at the appropriateness of the response.

"She was the most creative of the three. The other two... Well, you met Keera already," she said as if that explained it all.

"And is your third child older or younger?"

"Chalice is the oldest. She's twenty-three now."

A pretty young woman with a big Afro, lightened with hints of brown, appeared in the doorframe. She was sporting a pair of designer sunglasses and knee-high boots that made her look like she'd stepped right off the cover of *Rolling Stone*. "What's with the serious looking white woman?" she asked, eying Elle suspiciously over her aviator frames.

"Chalice!" Mrs. Biggs scolded, clearly more embarrassed than angry. "This is Detective Walker. She's here about Katie."

Chalice removed her glasses and set them down on the counter. "What about Katie?" she asked, looking more concerned than suspicious now.

"I just had a question for your mom." Elle drew the necklace from her jacket pocket and held it out in front of Mrs. Biggs. The little ladybug charm swung like a pendulum on its chain. There was no change in Mrs. Biggs's demeanor, at least none that Elle could detect. But Chalice was a different story. Her eyes grew wide, her jaw slack. She knew something.

"It's not Katie's, if that's what you're asking," Mrs. Biggs said.

"Did she like ladybugs or have something similar?" Elle asked more to Chalice than to Mrs. Biggs.

Mrs. Biggs shook her head. "Not that I know of."

"How about you, Chalice? Do you recognize the charm?"

The muscle in Chalice's jaw twitched. "No," she said and turned her attention to packing the notebook and highlighter pens into a leather satchel.

"You sure?" She didn't look up.

"It's not hers," Mrs. Biggs said once again. "I'd know if she had something like that."

Elle sensed that there was more to the story but knew better than to press the girl here. That might be the reason for her silence now. *Whatever she knows may be something she's afraid to say in front of her mother.*

"I'm sorry to have taken up your time." Elle carefully wound the necklace into a coil in her palm and put it back in her pocket. Chalice's eyes followed the movement.

"No trouble at all," Mrs. Biggs said, standing up to show Elle to the door.

"Please. You've been hospitable enough. And I've obviously interrupted your breakfast." She glanced at the cereal bowl just to the right of the textbook. A few Os still floated on top of the unnaturally pink milk. "I can show myself out." She hoped Chalice would see that as the invitation it was and follow her to her car—pass her a note or whisper something like in the movies.

She didn't because this wasn't a movie. And it wasn't going to be as easy as that. Elle checked the dashboard clock. In less than five hours, Alia would have been gone twelve days. She knew the statistics. Ninety-four percent of abducted children are found alive within the first seventy-two hours. After that, "it's hope for the best but expect the worst." The chances of Alia being found alive now were slim to none. Elle squeezed the ladybug charm in her pocket hoping that it would bring her—and this case—a little superstitious luck.

CHAPTER THIRTEEN

Maddie Burch sat across from Loraine Holbrook, Ed Kandinsky's high school sweetheart. She could still see remnants of the cheer captain despite the wrinkles, the extra weight, and the gray roots that made her mousy brown head of hair look like the snow-capped Andes Mountains.

Maddie had started researching Ed when Elle had first dropped his name—the "jackass" straddling the fence between superhero and retiree running lead on the Ambrois case. From the stories Elle told, the guy should be facing a sexual harassment suit big enough to prevent him from ever seeing a dime of his pension. But then, the precinct was a good ol' boys club, where they'd probably mistake EEO, Equal Employment Opportunity, for a cable channel. Her interest in Ed wasn't the sexual harassment angle, not that she wouldn't mind writing that story. But right now she was much more interested in whether he was working with the Copelands—*for* the Copelands, more like it.

When Elle brought the ladybug necklace to Kandinsky, not only didn't he follow up with the Ambrois family, but he mocked her in front of all of her colleagues.

Maddie hated Kandinsky for his treatment of women, especially Elle. If she could prove he had a connection to Boone's family, she might be able to get him thrown off the Ambrois case. That was why she was currently sitting in Loraine Holbrook's kitchen.

Judging by the matching canister set and breadbox, the little frilly throw pillows on the bench, and one of those designer dogs—sproodle doodle or whatever—following Loraine wherever she went, Mrs. Holbrooke was the Suzy Homemaker type, that is, if Suzy Homemaker had a French manicure and a rock on her finger the size of Gibraltar.

"I haven't thought about Eddie in years," she said, pouring coffee into a mug that read, *It's been Monday all week.* "You sure you don't want a cup?"

"No thank you." Maddie avoided the stuff. She had enough trouble sleeping without Elly to add caffeine to the mix. "So back then people around town thought of you two as *the* couple—homecoming king and queen, right?"

"Yes, we were." She smiled politely—a little too polite. Maddie sensed she was hiding something. "There's a picture of us in the yearbook."

"I'd love to see it."

Loraine and her designer dog accessory disappeared into the living room. When she returned, she was carrying a navy blue book; on its cover was the year 1970 in big bubble letters enclosed in white falcon wings. She flipped through the pages.

"Here it is," she said, her finger marking the photo. "You can't tell in the black and white picture, but his tie matched his car, not my dress. It was a cute pink lace overlay number that I bought at JC Penney's."

The picture featured the couple sitting in an old hardtop with chrome headliners and spears on the front fender. "That's vintage, right?"

Loraine nodded. "A 1957 Chevy Bel Air." She laughed. "He talked about it so much that forty years later I can still remember the names of the paint colors: Pinecrest Green and India Ivory."

"Do you mind if I take a picture for the story?" That's how she'd gotten into Loraine's house—on the pretext she was writing a story on Greenfield High's Class of 1970.

"Be my guest."

Maddie snapped a picture of the yearbook page with her phone. The caption under the photo read, "Couple most likely to get married."

"Obviously you didn't stay together."

Loraine looked away. She straightened against the chair back. "No," she said, closing the book abruptly.

"What happened?"

Something changed behind Loraine's eyes. Even though her lips were fixed in the same polite smile, there was a slight twitch in her bottom lip and a tightening in her jaw muscles that told Maddie she'd hit a nerve.

"My goodness, look at the time," Loraine said and stood. "I hate to rush you off, but I have a mahjong group coming at four and I still have to get the hors d'oeuvres ready."

"Mrs. Holbrook, do you remember Ed being friends with any of the Copelands?"

"The who?"

"The Copelands—Richard or Marie?"

"Isn't that the rich family who has the charity ball every year at Christmas?" Maddie nodded. "They didn't go to Greenfield. I don't think Ed knew them."

"So the breakup between you and Ed…"

Loraine's pace toward the door quickened. "I really have to—"

"Was he cheating on you? Is that what ended your relationship?"

"No, he didn't cheat on me." She swallowed.

"What then?"

"It was a long time ago. It doesn't matter anymore."

"What happened? Off the record."

Loraine studied her for a moment, as if sizing her up. "He…
He forced himself on me." She frowned. "But it was a different
time then. Boys will be boys, you know?"

Maddie was shocked. This wasn't what she'd expected.

"Did you go to the police?"

Loraine shook her head. "It was 1970. Date rape wasn't
even a thing." Loraine brushed her bangs out of her eyes and
opened the door. She obviously wanted Maddie to leave. And
Maddie wanted to leave. She felt terrible for having brought the
whole thing up. "I'm sorry," she managed before the door closed
behind her.

If Chalice's Facebook profile was accurate, she worked at
the LOFT Outlet store at Riverwalk. Elle and the girls were
on their way there now. Elle figured that Chalice was more
likely to open up to someone closer to her age. And given the
white woman comment, the fact that Shae was a person of color
couldn't hurt.

The car ride was unusually quiet. Elle noticed in the rearview
that the girls were seated on opposite sides of the backseat
bench, as if avoiding contagion from each other. This was not
what she was expecting after finding the Prius's windows fogged
up and the two of them with matching guilty expressions sitting
so closely that they might as well have been in each other's
laps. Hell, she half expected they'd be planning their wedding
reception dinner or on a search for a U-Haul rental place by
now.

"You girls okay?"

"We're fine," Fern said too quickly, her gaze on the window
rather than Elle.

Shae's eyes met Elle's in the rearview mirror. Her right brow
hitched up slightly. It was an expression that Elle interpreted as
sarcasm, as if to say, "If she says so."

The Outdoor Collection at Riverwalk was an indoor outlet
mall in downtown New Orleans. The marketplace boasted
seventy-five upscale retailers, including Nordstrom, Kenneth

Cole, and Steve Madden, as well as several restaurants and counter-serve eateries. Elle was never one for shopping or for the kind of communal fast food indicative of food courts. Malls actually made her lymph nodes swell. She couldn't help but scowl as they emerged from the skywalk into the throngs of Independence Day sale shoppers. In the storefront windows were emaciated mannequins in red, white, and blue striped scarves and skintight jeans embroidered with the stars and stripes to encourage the passersby to charge up their plastic in some pledge to patriotism. Thank goodness the LOFT was only a few stores down from the skywalk entrance.

Elle spotted Chalice's hair first—its autumnal browns stood out amongst the summer colors. "That's her," she said, elbowing Shae. She looked around for Fern but couldn't find her.

"She's trying on boots," Shae whispered, answering Elle's question before it had even been asked.

Chalice's exaggerated eye roll as they approached said that she recognized Elle. "What are you doing here?" she asked, sending a quick glance in Shae's direction.

"I thought you might be able to spare a moment to speak to us. It's about your sister."

"I'm Shae." Shae reached a hand toward Chalice in greeting.

Chalice ignored the gesture. "So," she said to Elle, "you brought a black girl along because you thought that would get me to talk?"

"Of course not. Don't be silly," she said feigning offense. "Shae's helping with the investigation."

Chalice glanced at Elle, Shae, and then her watch. "I have a fifteen-minute break coming up," she said. "You can buy me a smoothie."

"Deal."

The smoothie was thick and bright green. Even dressed up with an orange slice, a half of a strawberry, and a pretty pink-swirled straw, it still looked like toxic waste to Elle. She could barely stomach watching the girl drink it.

"So, the other day—"

"You want to know about the necklace, right?"

Well, that was easier than she thought. "Yes, did you recognize it?"

"No," she said, shaking her head.

"Nothing about it is familiar?"

"No, I've never seen that necklace before in my life." She took another swallow of the toxic waste. "So I dated this guy—a few years ago, before Katie's…death. Anyway, he used to call her Bug. It was a pet name. And sometimes he'd buy her little gifts, trinkets and stuff with cute little bugs on them."

"Ladybugs?"

"Not always, but yeah, once. It was a key chain or a purse charm, or something like that. She hung it off her backpack zipper."

"What guy was this?"

Chalice shook her head. "I can't tell you that."

"Why can't you?"

"His parents were… Let's just say that they weren't too happy when they found out that we were dating."

"So?"

"About a month before Katie disappeared, my boyfriend's racist brother told on us. His parents freaked, as you can imagine. They forbid him to see me. Guess I'm not the right breeding or whatever," she said, more to Shae than to Elle. "Anyway, they came to see my mother."

"His parents?" Chalice nodded. "What for?"

"What do you think? To threaten her of course."

"Threaten her why?"

"This family. They've got a reputation around here. Dating a black girl from this side of the tracks doesn't fit with that reputation, if you know what I mean."

Elle swallowed hard. "Was it Boone Copeland?"

Chalice bit her bottom lip. "How is this going to help Katie's case?"

"Look, I'm going to be honest with you, Chalice. We're investigating the disappearance of Alia Ambrois."

"The girl from the news?"

"Yes. I can't explain how, not yet anyway, but your cooperation right now might help us find her. Alive."

Chalice looked at Shae for confirmation. Shae nodded.

"All right," she said after a beat. "If it will help." She used her napkin to blot the condensation ring left on the table from her Styrofoam cup. "It was Boone."

"Did you stop dating after the parents came to visit?"

"Officially, yeah. But we were still seeing each other for a while."

"Did you ever sneak him in at night? Did he maybe climb through your bedroom window after your parents went to bed?"

Chalice shrugged. "Yeah, a couple times."

Elle pulled up the image on her phone. "Does this spot by the river mean anything to you?

Chalice squinted. "Oh my god! Yes! We used to all go fishing there by the river."

"With Katie?"

"Yes, why?"

"Chalice, do you think Boone could have hurt Katie?"

"*God no!*" she said taken aback. "He loved Katie! I mean there were times when I wasn't sure which one of us he was dating." She laughed. Elle's concerned expression made her smile fade. "Oh, not like that. That sounded terrible. I just meant that he loved spending time with her, like she was his own baby sister."

CHAPTER FOURTEEN

"But if Chalice is right and Boone didn't have anything to do with Katie's disappearance, why the weird trip to the river?" Fern asked, looking just as confused as Shae felt.

"What about interviewing Boone?" Shae offered.

Elle shook her head. "The Chief made it clear that Boone's not a suspect."

"Maybe Yasmine can help."

"Who?" Fern and Elle asked in unison.

Lilith greeted them at the door. Of course she had been expecting them. She looked the same. In fact, Shae was pretty sure that Lilith was dressed in the same outfit she wore on their first visit. The only change was that the tiny solar systems on Lilith's toenails had transformed into cartoon butterflies.

Anxious to get started, Shae scooped up the stones in her fist before Lilith had a chance to remind her of their purposes.

"Yes, let's make haste." Lilith took a seat across from Shae at the table and held out her hands.

Shae laid her palms on Lilith's and waited for the whale sounds to commence.

There wasn't much chanting before she was spiraling in a familiar funnel cloud. She braced herself for impact. She did slam into something hard, but it wasn't the road. It was concrete. She opened her eyes to find that she was sprawled across the concrete steps of a building with a domed ceiling and pillars. She pulled herself erect, her eyes falling on a marble Lady Justice statue that sat atop the dome like a star on a Christmas tree. *A courthouse?*

"Well, hello, stranger."

Shae turned at the sound. "Yasmine."

"At your service." Yasmine did a little bow, her plump lips curling into a smile.

"Were you able to find anything out about Katie Biggs?"

Yasmine squinted up at the marble statue. "Blind justice." She shook her head. "Not likely." She sniffed the air.

"What is it?"

"Wet dog." She grimaced.

Before Shae had an opportunity to look for the dog, he was bounding toward her. It was the husky. She recognized him by his two-toned eyes. His fur hung in wet tendrils as if he'd just come from a swim in a lake.

He didn't stop at Shae, though, but instead ran past her, up the steps to the large ornately decorated courthouse doors. He sat on his haunches and wagged.

Yasmine folded her arms. "Way to steal the show," she said to him.

Shae had barely opened the doors enough to see what was inside before he raced in. They found him in an aisle of the jury box, his wet chin propped up on one of the bench seats.

"What're you trying to tell me?" Shae asked. "I don't understand."

"I don't either." Yasmine squinted at him. "I did find a memory, though."

"What?"

"I told you I'd go searching for anything that might help you with your Katherine Biggs gravestone." Yasmine pushed a fallen hair behind her ear with her finger. "Well, I found one of her memories."

"What do you mean you found a memory?"

"Sometimes when people die, their memories get lost. We've got libraries full of lost memories separated from their owners. And, sure enough, one of your girl's memories is here."

"Does it have something to do with a court or a jury?"

Yasmine shrugged. The husky barked as if in protest. "Well, maybe he knows something I don't."

"What happens in this memory?"

Yasmine drew a square in the air with her finger. "See for yourself." When she'd closed the square, its interior turned black as if she had cut out the scenery. And then a movie scene filled the square.

A black girl sat on a patch of grass on the edge of the water. She was holding a fishing rod. Boone Copeland knelt next to her and worked at disentangling her rod's knotted fishing line.

"Some kids are picking on me at school." She used her free hand to pluck up some blades of grass.

He let the line fall and turned his full attention to the girl. "How are they picking on you, Bug?"

"You know," she said sheepishly. "Just being mean and stuff."

He seemed to consider this. "Did you tell your mom?"

"I'm telling *you*." Her lips puckered into a pout.

"I'm glad you told me." He wrapped an arm around her shoulder. "I promise you, Bug, that I'll protect you from anybody who tries to hurt you."

The square fell dark.

"I don't know if it's use—" Yasmine stopped talking when both she and Shae's attention was drawn back to the square, now lit with a new scene. This time it was Boone by himself, kneeling by the same riverbed.

Yasmine squinted at the image. "I haven't seen this. This isn't part of the memory."

"Where's it from then?"

The husky shook, water droplets flying off his fur with the movement.

"I guess from him." Yasmine used the corner of her blouse to blot her now wet arm. She brought the fabric to her nose. "River water?"

"I couldn't protect you," Boone said to the water. "I broke my promise, Bug, and I'm sorry." He lay something on the ground. It glinted in the moonlight.

The ladybug necklace. Shae swallowed hard. "It's not him," she said aloud.

"What?" Yasmine blinked.

"Boone." Shae felt for the stone in her pocket. She tried to explain that she had to get back but she was already on her way before the words were out.

CHAPTER FIFTEEN

Fern and Shae arrived home from Lilith's late that evening. As they already had plans to meet up with the detective and reporter in the morning, they didn't call them to share what they'd learned. Instead, they drove home in silence. Fern guessed Shae was feeling the same thing as her, defeated. With Boone ruled out as a suspect, they didn't have much of anything. And it was even less likely that they'd find Alia now. Of course it wasn't just Alia that was upsetting Fern.

Even the sight of her reflection in the mirror dressed in the new leather zip-side knee high boots she'd bought at the LOFT didn't make Fern happy. Cute and a whole inch taller, but still unhappy.

"What's up?" Ruby popped her head of gray hair into the doorframe. "Whoo-ee!" She whistled through her teeth, "Those boots are made for walkin'!"

"I don't feel much like walking." She plopped down on the bed and unfastened the buckles.

"Do I sense buyer's remorse?" Ruby scooped up some tissue paper that had fallen out of the shoebox when Fern was unpacking.

"It's not the boots."

"What is it then?"

Fern's eyes welled with tears.

"Oh, honey. What's happened?"

It used to be that when she'd had a bad day, she could make herself feel better by buying a new outfit, a new CD, a new thing. Now, those very same things made her feel worse—not better. She kicked off the boots. Without her calves to hold them up, they slumped to the ground as if they somehow knew they had failed her.

She thought of how hard Shae and Mrs. Williams were struggling to hold onto the farm. And she thought of how she thought so little of money that she could drop a hundred and eighty dollars on boots as some sort of therapy. The contrast made her sick to her stomach. She'd gone to summer camp every year since she was eight. Like her friends, her tuition and her bills were paid for. She'd had her own car since before she could drive, and despite some unpaid internships, she'd never worked a day in her life. Everything had come easily to her. It was as if she'd been born with invisible visas and passports that allowed her to navigate the world with an ease that Shae had probably never known.

She felt ashamed—ashamed of her defensiveness about the stupid door knocker, ashamed of her disparaging comments about community college, ashamed of who she'd been...before Shae. "I feel like I don't know who I am anymore."

Ruby sat down next to her on the bed. "What do you mean?"

"You remember what you said about the kaleidoscope—about how if you look at something differently, you know, it changes?"

Ruby nodded.

"I feel like everything changed."

"How do you mean?"

"I don't know. I just…" *I've just been so stupid.*

"We don't know what we don't know," Ruby said as if reading her mind.

Fern thought then of that moment in the car—the moment she and Shae had almost kissed. Ruby was right. She didn't know what she didn't know. "Do you think someone could live their whole life thinking something about themselves that isn't true?"

"I don't think that it's as black and white as that. We're complex creatures, Fern. And our lives are full of metamorphoses." She brushed some hair behind Fern's ear. "You've just turned the kaleidoscope and the petals have become swirls and the swirls have become stars. Take a look at those stars." Ruby tilted her head back as if they were there on the ceiling. "Aren't those stars beautiful?"

Yes. They are beautiful.

* * *

Ms. Burch, Detective Walker, and the girls had agreed to meet at the diner the next day. "To regroup," Detective Walker had said on the phone. Shae was happy about the invitation, given that she still had yet to fill the detective and Ms. Burch in on the Boone revelation.

It was clear to Shae that something with Fern had changed. She wasn't avoiding eye contact. In fact, her gaze seemed fixed on Shae with an imaginary string. And Fern had scooted so far into the booth that Shae imagined she could feel all 98.6 degrees radiating off her. *Or maybe that's my own temperature? Is it hot in here?*

"Shae, earth to Shae." Apparently, Detective Walker was talking to her.

"Sorry, what?" Fern's proximity was scrambling her brains. She fanned herself with her menu.

Walker exhaled noisily and tapped her pen against the table. She was clearly annoyed. "We were talking about the trees you said you saw in the distance…"

Shae felt Fern scoot closer, her thigh now pressing against her own. She was having trouble focusing.

"Do you remember what kind of trees they were? We might be able to place it if we know the species of trees."

"I didn't get a good look at them. I was running."

"Running where?"

"To the barn."

Ms. Walker's eyes passed over the yellow legal pad in front of her. "A garage that looked like a barn," she read, her pen marking the place. "How do you know it was a garage?"

"There was a car in it."

Walker's eyes widened. "You saw a car?"

"The side of it, yeah. It was covered in a tarp mostly."

"What kind of car? Did you catch any of the plate?"

"No plate, but it was one of those vintage deals. Blue-green."

"Sixties vintage?"

Shae shook her head. "I don't know. Like James Dean time."

"A Bel Air?" Madeline Burch practically shouted this, making the diners at the surrounding tables stop their conversations and turn in their direction. The reporter fumbled with her phone. "I have a picture." She swiped through the images. "Here!" She held the phone out to Shae.

It was a picture of a black and white photograph of a young man and woman in the very same style car she'd glimpsed in the barn.

"That's it! I don't believe it! How did you know?"

Walker leaned closer to inspect the fuzzy image on the reporter's phone. "Where'd you get that?"

"Loraine Holbrook's yearbook. The Falcons. Class of 1970. Loraine is Ed Kandinsky's high school sweetheart."

"My Ed Kandinsky?" Walker asked, her eyes widening in surprise.

Burch nodded. "*Your* Ed Kandinsky. I was doing a little digging," she explained. "Given how dismissive he's been of Boone's involvement, I thought he might have some ties to the Copelands."

"Does he?"

"Not that I can tell." Burch leaned closer. "But he's definitely more of an asshole than you think."

"Is that even possible?" Walker laughed.

Fern, who had up until this point been silent, tapped her spoon against her mug as if she were about to make a toast. "Can someone tell us who Ed Kandinsky is?"

"He's a detective in Elly's department," Burch said.

"Not just a detective. He's lead on the Ambrois case." Walker sat back in her seat, looking defeated. "He's lead. If he's involved somehow…"

"Do you have a picture of him?" Burch asked.

Walker picked up her phone. She cycled through her photos. "Here's one," she said as if surprised to find it. "From the police-fire softball tournament."

The picture was of an overweight guy in a pinstriped baseball jersey. The fabric was so stretched at the buttons that Shae wouldn't be surprised if one popped off and blinded the photographer. The man's hair was salt and pepper—white around the temples—and he had a walrus style mustache under which his lips disappeared.

"That's not him. Red Handkerchief guy is way younger. And fitter."

"Like Boone." Burch signaled the waitress.

Shae wasn't sure if it was a statement or a question. "Boone didn't do it."

Burch straightened in her chair.

"I saw Katie's memory in the Alter Plane."

"The what?"

"It doesn't matter. Just trust me that it's not Boone. The ladybug necklace wasn't a trophy. It was more of a symbol of his guilt over not having protected her."

Burch's eyebrows couldn't have been any higher on her forehead.

"But yeah," Shae continued, "the man was closer to Boone's age than this Kandinsky guy." The details were fuzzy now. It was like trying to recall a dream a couple days after having it.

"Well, that doesn't mean Kandinsky *isn't* involved," Walker offered.

"What's next then?" Shae asked. "More stakeouts?"

"We need to find out if Kandinsky still has that car. If he does, we need to know where he keeps it."

"How?" Burch asked. "You said that the chief made it clear that—"

"Carefully." She sat back in her chair. "No, you know what?" she said as if a thought had just occurred to her. "I'm not going to be so concerned about my job that I lose sight of what's important. *Again.*"

A look passed between Walker and Burch—a look that Shae felt but didn't understand. It felt like an apology.

"We're going to find Alia," Walker continued, "and I don't care if I'm a detective when we do."

CHAPTER SIXTEEN

Elle tried to look casual despite the fact that making conversation with Kandinsky was just about the least casual thing she could do. She stood just behind his desk, considering how she might strike up a conversation with a sexist bigoted asshole—an asshole, who, according to Maddie, was also a rapist.

"What the hell do you want, Walker?" he bellowed, despite the fact that she wasn't standing in his view.

She stepped closer. "I was just noticing your calendar." The month of July featured a shiny red convertible with chrome star trim. "That's a beauty, huh?" *Way to go, Elle. That was a completely normal thing for you to say.*

Kandinsky's eyes followed her gaze. "1955 Pontiac Star Chief. Same car Lucy and Ricky drove to the West Coast." He squinted at her, as if suddenly realizing that he hated her. "A dyke into cars? You couldn't be more cliché if you tried, Walker."

Elle bit her tongue. "Yeah, right," she said and forced a laugh. "So, I heard some of the guys saying that you restore old cars."

Kandinsky snapped the folder closed in front of him. "Again, what do you want, Walker?"

"I have this nephew who's looking to restore an old Chevy Bel Air and I heard that you—"

"What year?" he interrupted, his scowl slackening.

"Um. 1957, I think."

"Color?"

"Blue-green."

"Pinecrest green?"

"Yeah, that might be it." *He's hooked. Reel him in, Elle. Reel him in.*

"Well, I'll be damned!" he said. "I had that exact model!" He was smiling now. Elle was pretty sure that was the first time she'd seen his teeth.

"No kidding!" *I want to thank the Academy...*

"I did a complete body off restoration. Rebuilt the turbo four-o-four speed automatic transmission with overdrive. You should've heard her purr! And she had all the original body panels and— "

"You still have her?" *Your impatience is showing.* "I mean she sounds awesome," Elle said, trying to save face. "I'm sure my nephew would love to see her."

"Wish I did." He leaned back in his chair so that the two front legs lifted off the ground an inch or so. "She'd be worth a pretty penny right now. I'd be retiring in Cabo if I'd kept her," he said wistfully. "How did your nephew get one?"

"Uh . . . a car show I think. Did you sell yours?"

He shook his head. "A pair of bitches in the pocket..." *Bitches, what? What the hell was he talking about?* "Lost her to a flush. Can you fucking believe it?"

"A poker game? You lost the car in a poker game?"

"When you're dealt bitches, Walker, you raise. That's what you do."

"You remember who won?"

"Hell, yes, I remember! That asshole Deats rode all around town, showing her off as if he'd done the work on her, as if he'd bagged groceries for a whole summer just to replace the damn steering wheel..."

As Kandinsky cataloged every minute little repair and purchase down to the floor mats, Elle was busy trying to remember why the name Deats was so familiar to her. And then it hit her. *Deats Meats. The guy who killed Tyrell Lewis.* "The butcher?"

Kandinsky nodded. "Who knows where she is now. The state probably repossessed her when the family went bankrupt after the trial." Kandinsky pushed a pad toward Elle with his elbow. "Leave his number for me."

"Whose number?"

He eyed her suspiciously. "Your nephew's."

"Oh, yeah. Right." She picked up the pen.

"What the hell is this?" Someone said from behind her. "k.d. Lang asking for advice on how to please a woman without the proper plumbing?" The sound of Santos's Muttley snicker made Elle grind her teeth.

Kandinsky's mustache lifted into a half-moon, his eyes on Elle. "There's no comparing to the real thing," he said and laughed.

"It's a shame that this is the only way you boys know how to use your tongues," she said. "Guess that's why I have such a hard time getting your wives out of my bed." She turned to leave.

"Bitch!" he called after her.

"*Dick*," she mumbled. A young female rookie in blues frowned at Elle sympathetically as she made her way to her desk.

Back in her cubicle, she ran a title search in the National Motor Vehicle Database for the car Kandinsky had lost to Clifford Deats. There was only one record of a title transfer. At least on paper, the Bel Air still belonged to the Deats family.

That afternoon, the girls and Elle met at what was becoming *their* diner booth and Elle shared her conversation with Kandinsky. Shae dipped a crinkle cut French fry into the lake of ketchup on her plate. "I know his kids—Marshall and Mandy. They went to my school." Just before she closed her teeth around the ketchup-smeared end, the fry disappeared. Like a seagull on a tourist, Fern swooped in and stole it.

"Hey!" Shae protested.

She chewed, her lips curled into a smile.

Elle was happy to see that they were getting along again.

"Sorry I'm late." Maddie eased her arms out of the sleeves of her purple raincoat. A strip of ridiculous rubber ducks decorated the lapels and cuffs. "Traffic," she said as she scooted into the booth next to Elle. It was a wrap-around booth large enough to seat six, giving Maddie her choice of spots. But she picked this one—right next to Elle—and then she smiled. It had been too long since Elle had seen that smile. It made her heart skip a beat.

"So, catch me up." Maddie used her napkin to blot her cheeks and neck, still damp from the rain. Elle couldn't help but think of the many other times she'd seen Maddie's skin glisten with a sheen of perspiration, worked up by hours of lovemaking.

"We were just talking about Kandinsky's car," she said, trying to shake the warmth left by the memory. "Shae knows the Deats kids." She looked at Shae. "Do you think you could ask Marshall and—?"

"I'll ask Mandy about it, but Marshall… He and I don't get along."

"Why not?"

"Let's just say that he doesn't like people who look like me."

Katie Biggs and Alia Ambrois are both black, Elle reminded herself. "Is the family racist?"

"I don't think Mandy is, but Marshall would clothe himself in a Dixie flag if he could. Been that way ever since his father's trial."

"So what happened to his father?" Fern asked.

"Mr. Deats was found guilty."

"Of manslaughter," Maddie added. "With a pretty hefty sentence—forty years."

"The Deatses were well to do before then, had a business and everything. They lost it all." Shae swirled a fry in the ketchup. "Anyway Marshall's been a Hitler-in-training ever since."

Marshall Deats. He was on Elle's radar now. "Tell you what? How about you girls visit with Mandy and find out what you can about that car, and Maddie and I will pay a visit to this Marshall character. Shae, do you know where he lives?"

"I know he owns a gator farm a few miles outside town."

CHAPTER SEVENTEEN

Fern tapped her thigh to the beat of the new Maroon 5 song that was playing on the car radio. Adam Levine was begging for some sugar or something. It wasn't that she was enjoying the song, let alone even hearing it. She was too busy trying to think of a way to bring up the subject with Shae. *The* subject with a capital *T*. She kept thinking about the stars Ruby mentioned.

"Did you hear about the Clifford Deats trial in New York?" Shae pushed the lever on the steering column to signal a turn.

"No, I don't think so." Fern glanced at Shae but quickly turned away. She was having trouble looking at her, especially when Shae looked back. Anytime Shae looked at her, she felt like she could feel her eyes on her skin.

"Are you mad at me, Fern?"

"What? No, of course not. Why would I be mad?"

"I know it must be weird for you, finding out that your best friend from childhood turned out to be gay." Shae smiled an uneasy kind of smile. "It doesn't say anything about you, you know."

"Maybe it does." It was out before she had time to plan what she was going to say next.

Shae turned to look at her then, and she fought the instinct to turn away.

"I might have thought about it."

Shae shrugged. "I think everybody thinks about it. It doesn't mean—"

"I might be thinking about it more lately." She closed her eyes. She couldn't look at her and say it. "I might be thinking about you...like that." She felt the car pull to a stop.

"What are you saying?"

"I thought you were going to kiss me the other day in the car." She exhaled a slow breath. "The thing is... I wanted you to. I really wanted you to. And it's all can think about now. It's like I'm seeing things differently—things from my past. And I think... I don't know." Embarrassed, she covered her eyes with her hands. "This isn't coming out right."

She felt Shae's fingers peel hers away from her face.

"This is going to sound crazy," Shae said, "but I'm pretty sure I've been in love with you all of my life."

Shae was close enough now to smell the peppermint of her shampoo. It made her head swim.

Without saying anything, Shae pressed her lips to Fern's. It was a soft little kiss, barely a kiss, but Fern thought she could feel it in every cell of her body. When she opened her eyes, Shae's expression had changed. She looked afraid, as if she half expected Fern to slap her or run from the vehicle.

"Was that...okay?" Shae asked. "Are you regretting—"

Before Shae could finish the sentence, Fern had grabbed hold of her jacket and pulled her into another embrace. This kiss wasn't soft or meek. It was hungry and passionate. She wasn't sure but she might have moaned into Shae's mouth.

As they walked up the concrete steps to Mandy Deats's apartment, Shae watched Fern's backside. She was wearing a short denim skirt with a zipper up the back. *My god, that skirt.* Shae had to restrain herself from letting her mind wander...

wander underneath that fabric, where she could imagine pushing Fern's panties to the side with her fingers.

She'd never been more turned on by a kiss. When Fern's tongue had slipped into her mouth like that, she thought she would burn to ash right there in her seat. Hell, the whole car should have burst into flames the way she was feeling. It was a miracle she could still use her legs.

Mandy Deats opened the door wearing a faded UL Cajuns hoodie and a pair of stone-washed jeans. She was heavier and more tired looking than Shae remembered. Half circles of pale skin hung limply like saddlebags under her bloodshot eyes.

"Yeah?" she asked, without even a hello, the unmistakable smells of liquor and cigarettes floated on the question.

"Hi Mandy," Shae said. "How've you been?"

"Who the hell are you?"

"It's Shae. Shae Williams." Mandy didn't look as if the name meant anything to her. "We went to Greenfield together. Remember?"

Mandy looked Shae up and down in an exaggerated gesture, her whole head moving, not just her eyes. "Yeah, so?" she asked. "What do you want?"

While Mandy and Shae weren't the best of friends in high school, they had hung out in the girls' bathroom smoking cigarettes and talking about teenager things like music and fashion, so Shae had expected the reunion to be less icy.

"We were hoping we could chat with you for a few minutes." Shae could see some kids' toys strewn around the carpet in the foyer—a plastic train, a miniature football. She couldn't help but hope there was someone else there to care for the kids. *Who drinks at one o'clock in the afternoon on a Tuesday?*

"About what?"

"We were wondering if you could help us track down a car, a car that your father owned."

Mandy tapped her foot in irritation.

"A green Chevy Bel Air."

She squinted at Shae—both eyes reduced to tiny dark slits—the white all but disappeared. "Why do you want to know about that?"

"We heard that your father won it in a poker game, and we were curious if it was still in the family."

Her eyes darted to Fern, as if she'd just noticed she was there. "And who are you?"

"Sorry, I'm Fern Beaumont." Fern reached out her hand. Mandy didn't take it.

"Fine. Whatever," she said, as if exhausted by the conversation. "You have five minutes."

They followed her into the kitchen.

"Mom!" A toddler's disembodied voice crashed into the room like a cannon.

"One more word, Joshua, and no dinner! I mean it!"

Shae and Fern exchanged uncomfortable glances.

"You can just move that stuff," she said, her eyes on the magazines, lottery scratch-offs, and a mountain of cellophane candy wrappers on the couch cushions.

"So," Shae said, pushing the magazines to the side to make room to sit. "Do you remember the car?"

"Yeah, I remember it." Mandy picked up a coffee mug, its rim smeared with lipstick despite the fact that she wasn't wearing any. She took a healthy swig—a swig too large for coffee or anything hot for that matter.

"Do you own it now?"

"Do I look like I own a vintage car?" she said and laughed at her own joke, her laugh devolving into a hacking cough. She reached for a packet of cigarettes.

"Did you sell it?"

Mandy struggled with the lighter, striking the pinwheel several times before a flame finally lit long enough to get her cigarette smoking. "Since I live in this beautiful palace here..." She held up her hands as if to show off the secondhand furniture and the stained carpets. "Dad thought my brother Marshall should get it, along with anything else he managed to hide from the creditors." She exhaled two streams of smoke from her nostrils as she spoke.

"Does he still have it?"

"Fuck if I know."

"You don't stay in contact with him?"

"We haven't spoken for over a year, not even at dad's funeral."

"I was sorry to hear about that," Shae said.

"Why?" Mandy sucked on her cigarette, the end burning red.

Shae straightened in her seat. "I know how devastating it is to lose a parent. I lost my father two years ago."

"I'm glad Dad is gone."

She waited for lightning to strike.

"Why do you say that?" Fern asked.

Mandy took a swig from the coffee mug again. "Some people are reminders of things that you want to forget."

"Reminder of what?" Fern asked.

Mandy smashed the half-smoked cigarette into an overfilled ashtray. "I killed a boy," she said, her voice hollow like tree branches in winter.

Shae, taken aback by the confession, shifted uncomfortably in her seat.

"Tyrell Lewis," she said. "That was his name. Tyrell Lewis." She swallowed another swig from the coffee mug.

"I thought he—"

"He didn't. He barely even knew me." She stared into the mug, her eyes glazed. "Tyrell Lewis," she said again. She set the mug down on the table and brushed her palms together as if ridding them of dirt or soot. "I couldn't tell him. Not after what he'd done to Tyrell."

"Who?"

"My father. He'd killed him. If I'd told him that I lied... Can you imagine what it would have done to him? My lie killed Tyrell." Mandy's eyes welled up with tears. Fern reached out to touch her hand, but she flinched away. "You should go," she said and reached for her cigarettes again.

Fern felt heavy with sadness as she sank into the passenger seat.

Shae latched her seatbelt. "She's punishing herself."

"What happened to Tyrell..." She shook her head. "It's horrifying."

They drove most of the way in silence. The radio was on but the volume was so low that the music sounded like hissing with a beat. Tyrell's story turned Fern's stomach. What happened to him would have never happened had Tyrell's skin been white like hers.

She used to say she was colorblind—that she didn't see race—that everyone was the same to her. *People are just people.* She'd said it too many times to count.

"I never really thought about us being different," she said. "I don't ever have to think about my race. I don't ever have to worry that someone wants to hurt me because of my race. I have no idea what that's like."

"It's not so great," Shae said, and laughed. The quiver of her chin contradicting the lighthearted tone.

She laced her fingers through Shae's and squeezed.

Shae glanced at Fern, her eyes watery. "I wish you weren't going home in August. I feel like we just found each other again."

Me too, Fern thought but didn't say, the lump in her throat making it too painful to speak.

CHAPTER EIGHTEEN

iPhone navigation led them down a tangle of dirt roads. Aside from an abandoned trailer and a rusted wheelbarrow in a field, there wasn't much around. Elle instinctively checked the gas tank—quarter-full—a reflex from driving in backwoods areas where the nearest gas station might as well have been in the next state.

The roads seemed to get narrower with each turn—this one almost completely eclipsed by weeds and underbrush except for two thick tire treads worn into its center. The only sign that marked the entrance to the farm was a metal square faded to a mint green, cautioning against swimming with or feeding the alligators.

"Does anyone really need to be told that?" Maddie asked, her eyes on the sign.

"You'd be surprised." Just four months earlier a 911 call came in from a resident at a senior living facility who had spotted a ten-foot-long gator with "a body in its jaws" on the golf course.

When they crested the next hill, the house came into view. It was a single-family American Craftsman with a brick porch and shingled roof. The siding was no longer white, brandishing dirt like a badge of the years it had weathered. The front lawn was the thirstiest Elle had ever seen, most of it a wiry brown hay that she imagined crunched like fall leaves under foot. Thick weeds had grown through the cracks in the concrete walk and front steps.

After the first knock, a dog practically attacked the bay window to their left, its saliva splattering the glass. Maddie, startled, stumbled backward into Elle's arms. Elle could smell her perfume, the scent making her dizzy. She knocked again. No answer.

"Let's check around back. Maybe he's working and can't hear us."

They rounded the house's perimeter to find a sea of open field, fenced off ponds to the east, and an old red barn to the west.

Elle's stomach seized when her eyes fixed on the roof of a small wooden shack. *It all congealed. The field. The barn. The shack.* Her hand went to her holster.

"Maddie, go back to the car," she said. She crouched down behind the corner lip of the house.

"What is it?"

"Just go back to the car. And lock the doors." Elle felt her phone vibrate in her pocket. A text from Shae: "It was Marshall's car. Don't know if he still has it. Mandy lied about Tyrell." She pulled her radio from her belt. "Code twenty," she said into the speaker. As she relayed the location, she followed Maddie just far enough to see that she made it safely into the car before turning back.

She knew if he was watching, she was a sitting duck with these open fields.

She drew her gun. "Police!" she shouted. She couldn't hear anything but some birds. She scanned the field for movement. Nothing. She made a run for the shack.

She knew by the casement windows. This was it. She cleared a circle in the glass with her palm. There, in the corner, she saw it. A tiny body—a child's body—curled into a ball like a kitten, half-hidden under a burlap sack. Elle couldn't tell if she was alive or dead. The door was secured with a padlock and a steel hasp. She'd have to go back to her car for bolt cutters. "Alia?" she said and knocked on the window.

The sack rustled, revealing one brown pigtail and a gnarly mess of hair on the other side where its twin used to be, and then a pair of dark brown eyes, wide like saucers.

"It's okay, Alia. I'm Detective Walker, with the police." She pushed her badge up to the glass.

The girl ran toward her. She pressed her hands to the glass. Elle did the same.

"I have to run to the car to get some cutters to get you out of here." She motioned to the driveway.

Elle could tell the girl was talking but couldn't make out the words. From the erratic way her mouth was moving and the panic in her eyes, Elle guessed she was asking her not to go.

"I'll be back in a minute. I promise." Elle flinched at the sound of a gun being cocked behind her.

"Now it's not nice to make promises you can't keep," a deep voice said.

Elle turned.

"Drop the pistol and put those pretty hands where I can see 'em."

Marshall was tall, muscular. He held the shotgun like a man confident in his aim.

"I'm a detective with Algiers Point PD," she said. "I've already called for back up. They'll be here any minute."

He tilted his head to the side like her father's dog did when he heard something rustling in the woods. "Don't hear no sirens."

"It's over, Marshall. If you let the girl go, we'll—"

"Girl? That's no girl. That there is a nigger."

Elle gritted her teeth and tried to focus on her training. "It's a kidnapping charge now. But if you hurt her, you could face the death penalty."

"Niggers have to pay."

"For what? What did Alia do to you?" She tried to use Alia's name as much as she could, knowing that if Marshall viewed her as a person, he would be less likely to hurt her.

"They destroyed my family. That boy hurt my sister and when the po-lice wouldn't do nothing, my father did. And what did he get for it? He was thrown in jail. Fucking nigger loving country!" He rammed the butt of his gun into the side of the shed, making Alia cry out in fear.

"Tyrell didn't hurt your sister, Marshall."

"You didn't see her! She had bruises on her ribs, her arms, her face. He—"

"No, *he* didn't do any of that. Your sister lied. It wasn't him."

"*Bullshit!*"

The gun shook in his hands and she worried that he might accidentally squeeze the trigger.

"Stop trying to get into my head."

"Call her. Ask her yourself." She reached her phone out to him but he made no move to take it. "There must be a reason you haven't hurt Alia. You don't want to hurt her, do you?"

"Collateral damage."

"What?"

"For juror number two." The muscle in his jaw flexed. "Her mother and that Biggs woman. They were the jurors that convicted him." His eyes grew dark. "Forty years was a death sentence."

Elle's eyes were drawn to movement in the brush behind him. A flash of strawberry blond hair. Maddie. *Keep him talking.* "Why not just kill Alia then? Why hold onto her?"

"If I kill her, they can grieve. But this way—" Marshall's words stopped short at the impact of the shovel with the back of his head. His skin went pale, the muscles in his cheeks slackened, and his jaw fell open. The gun dropped to the ground at his feet. Elle clambered for it. Disoriented, Marshall made no move to stop her. Instead, his whole body followed the movement of the gun; first, he buckled at the waist, then the knees. Then he crumpled to the ground like a deflated balloon. And there Maddie stood, eyes wide, her fingers gripping the handle of the shovel so hard that her knuckles were white.

Elle yanked Marshall's arms behind his back and secured the cuffs. He didn't resist, his arms like dead weight in her hands.

"Marshall Deats. You are under arrest for the murder of Katie Biggs and the kidnapping of Alia Ambrois. You have the right to remain silent…" She continued by rote while searching his pockets for the padlock key.

There was enough ammunition in the pockets of his shooting vest to start a revolution. The key was in an inside pocket sewn into the lining.

When she'd managed to unlock the door, the girl shot out as if spring-loaded and wrapped herself around Elle's thigh. She picked her up and held her to her chest. "You're safe," she said.

She could hear the sirens now. She cradled the girl in one arm and held her gun in the other. She watched over Marshall until the officers arrived on the scene. Several of them formed a makeshift circle around him as others inventoried the shack, the barn, and the house.

Elle made her way back to the car with Alia in her arms, noting the line of trees off in the distance, the red tobacco barn. It was all as Shae had described it.

CHAPTER NINETEEN

Chief McKinley pulled at his neck collar with his fingers. He was uncomfortable. "You said you had a lead and I..." It wasn't like him to avoid eye contact. "Well, if you'd've listened to me, we would have never found the girl alive." It was as close to an apology as Elle was going to get. "You'll need to let the family know the girls' names for the reward. I'm sure they'll want to organize a press release."

Elle had forgotten about the reward. "That's really going to help Shae's family."

"Well, good, I'm happy to hear it." He turned to go. He had almost reached his office door when he tossed it over his shoulder: "Nice work, Detective." The Chief rarely, if ever, offered compliments, so those three words made Elle's heart swell.

"Thank you, sir," she said aloud even though he was too far away to hear her.

She hadn't expected to find Maddie waiting for her outside the precinct, but there she was, dressed in a pastel blazer that reminded Elle of *Miami Vice*. It was a peach color that clashed with her hair. Elle couldn't stop the smile from forming. *Adorable.*

"Hey there, stranger."

"Hi." Maddie bit her bottom lip. "Do you have time to talk?"

Elle nodded, worried now at Maddie's seriousness. "Are you okay?"

"I want to apologize. You tried to tell me to let the Copeland thing go. I didn't listen." She swallowed. "I should have listened." After a beat, she continued, "What you said the other day, about losing sight of what's important... Were you talking about more than just the case?" Maddie's black frames slid a bit down her nose. She pushed them back up with her finger.

"Yes," Elle answered. "I was thinking about you when I said it. I was wrong, Maddie. You were more important than any title or any job. You were the most important thing in my life. I knew it the moment that you left. The first night I slept without you. And I know it now. Losing you was the worst mistake of my life. I would give it all back—I would resign—if it meant you'd come back to me."

"I need a story, Detective," Maddie said after a beat. "You have any idea where I can get one?"

Elle smiled. "As a matter of fact, I do. Have dinner with me, Madeline Burch of the *Ledger*. You'll get a good story out of it. I can promise you that."

Maddie stepped closer. Elle did the same. She didn't know if it was her or Maddie who initiated the kiss or if they had somehow met in the middle. It was a movie kiss, all breathless and clinging and sexy as hell. Elle couldn't stop her knee from parting Maddie's legs. There were hands in her hair, on her neck. Maddie's hands. Oh god, she loved kissing this woman. She could kiss this woman for hours...for days...for a lifetime...

And just as she thought that, Maddie broke free. Her green eyes were dark, darker than Elle remembered, her lips wet and swollen from kissing. "I've missed this," she said through labored breaths. "I've missed you."

Elle wanted to reach for her again. "I don't want to stop kissing you."

"I don't want to stop either." Maddie smiled a seductive smile that made Elle's knees weak. "But we are at the police station."

She glanced back at the building, half expecting it not to be there. The whole world seemed to have disappeared while they'd kissed. But the station *was* there. And Kandinsky was there, too, descending the steps with a box. He was officially retiring today, although not the way that he would have liked. It was a forced retirement with a severely slashed pension, the result of two female officers lodging sexual harassment complaints against him. When his eyes met Elle's, the corner of his mustache lifted into a sneer.

"What are they going to do," Elle asked loud enough for him to hear, "arrest us?" She pulled Maddie into another embrace and kissed her again—not wanting to ever let her go.

CHAPTER TWENTY

A half-full suitcase lay open on the little twin bed in the guest room that had been Fern's bedroom for the past two months. No matter how Fern positioned the boots, it was clear they weren't going to fit. *Just as well. I don't want them anyway.*

She slid the plane ticket to JFK into the front pocket of her messenger bag, wishing that she could jump into someone else's skin—someone who lived here—with Shae. Some part of her had known it the moment Shae had appeared in Ruby's living room on that first day looking all shy and adorable. Every part of her had known it the moment they'd kissed, parts she didn't even know she had. *I am in love with Shae.*

"Almost ready?" Ruby leaned her head into the doorframe.

"I guess."

"I have a little something for you to remember your summer here." Ruby held a shoebox wrapped in silver cellophane out to her.

"Thank you, Grandma."

"I made this one special for you."

She knew what it was of course. A kaleidoscope. Copper leaves wound their way around its circumference. "Are these fern fronds?" she asked touching one of the leaf's points.

"Yes."

She raised it to her eye. A solar system of purples, pinks, oranges, and blues came alive, the stars exploding into planets that collided and expanded with the movement of her fingers. She didn't know she was crying until she felt a drip fall onto her knee.

"What is it, honey?"

"The stars are so much more beautiful here," she said, still looking through the eyepiece.

Ruby wrapped an arm around her shoulder. "Sometimes we search for our futures and sometimes our futures find us."

She swallowed hard. "I don't want to leave, Grandma."

"You know you're welcome to stay here for as long as you like, Fernanda."

"But Mom and Dad—"

"This isn't their life. This is your life. These are your stars," she said, tapping a finger on the center of her chest.

She pulled the barn door open. The sound brought Shae's attention there. When she saw her, she dropped the rake she was holding and ran to her. She swept her up in her arms.

"I didn't think I'd get another chance to say goodbye, to breathe you in." She took a deep breath. "God, you smell good."

And before she could say anything, Shae's lips were on hers. And the world fell away—the way that it did in Shae's arms. When Shae released her, she felt dizzy, disoriented.

"What time are you leaving?" Shae glanced at her watch. "I could still drive you to the airport."

She had said no to the offer the first time, thinking it would be too hard to leave Shae at the security checkpoint and move farther and farther away until she couldn't see her anymore.

"How did it go with the financial advisor?"

"It's like a dream!" Shae smiled. "The reward money gave us enough to pay off most of the creditors. We're going to be able to keep the farm."

"I'm glad."

"And what about you? Are you looking forward to getting back to your friends?"

She took her hand. "I'm going to miss them."

"You mean you *have* missed them."

She shook her head. "No, I mean I *will* miss them. But it's better than missing you." She laced their fingers together. "I'm not leaving, Shae."

Shae blinked. "But Syracuse."

"There's Tulane. I could transfer."

"But—"

"But nothing. These are my stars."

"Your what?"

She shrugged. "It's something Ruby says."

"So you're really staying?"

"I'm really staying."

She saw it happen—a cloudiness like morning fog eclipsed Shae's eyes. And then… she was gone.

It was pitch black. Shae wasn't sure if her eyes were open or not. She was laying on her back, her legs stretched to their full length, her arms at her sides. She tried to sit up and slammed her head into a wall. There was about a foot of space between her and the ceiling. She felt with her hands. Walls on all sides of her. She was in a box. Adrenaline coursed through her body. Her heart raced. Her breath quickened. *A coffin! She was in a coffin!* She felt panicked and clawed at the seams in the walls.

Something rained down on the top of the box—rocks, dirt. *Oh my god!* She was being buried alive! She pounded on the ceiling with her fists. "I'm alive! I'm alive!" she shouted as loud as she could.

The shoveling stopped. There were voices, muffled voices. She strained to hear.

"Jesus Christ! We can't bury her alive."

"She'll be dead soon enough," another voice said. More dirt rained down on the box, some falling through the crack onto her face. She spit to try to get the taste out of her mouth.

There was a commotion then. Some shouting. A gunshot rang out. Something hard fell on the box and bounced.

A string of expletives followed. "Oh fuck, oh fuck, oh fuck!"

"Please? Let me out of here!" She kicked and pounded on the lid. "Let me out!"

Another thud. Then steps. The wood creaked under the weight. She could hear something heavy being pushed or rolled across the lid.

"Let me out! Please!" she shouted.

A piece of metal pushed through the seam between the lid and the side. A crowbar. He was using a crowbar to pry the lid open.

The sunlight was blinding. Her eyes were slow to adjust. When they did, she saw a billboard. A middle-aged woman holding an absurdly large check. The caption read, "Frank Newman Got Me $3 Million." The man's face came into view above her. He looked sweaty. Nervous. He had dark hair. Pockmarked cheeks. He reached a hand out to grab hold of her. A tattoo peeked out of the sleeve of his polo. The part she could see looked like a shark fin.

And then she heard it—far off in the distance—a familiar voice.

Fern's calling me.

Shae sat straight up, making Fern jump.

"We have a new assignment," she said.

Bella Books, Inc.

Women. Books. Even Better Together.

P.O. Box 10543
Tallahassee, FL 32302

Phone: 800-729-4992
www.bellabooks.com